BLACK SAGE

Center Point
Large Print

Also by L. P. Holmes and available from Center Point Large Print:

Singing Wires
Delta Deputy
Wild Summit

BLACK SAGE

L. P. Holmes

CENTER POINT LARGE PRINT
THORNDIKE, MAINE

This Center Point Large Print edition
is published in the year 2026 by arrangement with
Golden West Inc.

The text of this Large Print edition is unabridged.
In other aspects, this book may vary
from the original edition.
Printed in the United States of America
on permanent paper sourced using
environmentally responsible foresting methods.
Set in 16-point Times New Roman type.

ISBN: 979-8-90082-026-2

The Library of Congress has cataloged this record
under Library of Congress Control Number: 2026935574

Chapter I
THE ANCIENT HATE

At the crest of the trail that broke down by steep angles and abrupt switchbacks across the face of the Pahvant Rim, Reese Canby and Sandy Foss checked their horses and felt the hot breath of the desert washing up at them.

Here, the long drift of the piñon forest had thinned, giving way to the wide running curve of this barren red sandstone. A full five hundred feet below the desert began and spread its gray vastness away into hazy indefiniteness until, at what seemed the last edge of everything, the purple shadow which was the Garrison Hills lifted to anchor the world.

Sandy Foss rocked forward in his saddle, looking down at the loose outlines of the town of Cassadora that crouched below, there where the base of the rim and the first sweep of the desert met.

"Something I never could figure out, Reese. With all the state of Arizona to pick from, why would men want to build a town in a place like that? Hotter than the hinges. Nothing to see but a red rock rim in back and the everlasting desert in front. Give a man the jim-jams, living steady in Cassadora."

Reese Canby smiled briefly.

"Notice you never turn down a chance to ride in. There must be some attraction."

Sandy Foss colored boyishly. "Mary Stent," he said softly, "is one swell girl."

"On that, kid, we agree," Canby nodded. "But now that you've had a good look, what do you see?"

"I see Bert Lanifee's old red buckboard and about twice as much saddle bait as usual along the hitch rails," reported Sandy. "And there's a line of broncs tied along the fence of Pokey Carter's livery corral, most of 'em calicoes. Which means that Antone and some of his braves are in town. I guess the news that Henry Joel gave us was straight, Reese."

"Let's get on down," said Canby.

They went into the trail's steepness, their horses swinging deft and reaching forefeet while braking against the swift dropping slant with bunched haunches. Against the face of the rim, the heat was piled up thick, and Reese Canby felt the sweat start under his hatbrim.

They had come a long way, and fast, had these two, down from Reese Canby's summer range far up in the high valleys of the Chevron Mountains to the north. The mark of three months of rough living was on them, their clothes worn and ragged, the dark shadows of unshaven bristle along their jaws. But they were lean and hardy and fit, their eyes keen and clear, their faces dark from wind and sun.

Reese Canby was the bigger man, wider across the shoulders, taller in the saddle, and with a six-year bulge in age on his companion. This, added to the responsibility and authority of ranch ownership, laid certain lines of maturity about his mouth and chin. At times, he felt an almost paternal affection toward Sandy's gay and ebullient twenty-four years.

When the trail broke into the desert's flatness, the horses blew their relief and moved up to a jog, swinging into the west end of Dragoon Street, heading for the watering trough which stood under the overhang at the corner of the livery barn.

Across the street, Cap Lovelock showed in the door of his saddle shop, stood there a moment, then came on out across the hot dust.

"Don't know who I'd rather see show up," he said bluntly. "Get right along up to the courthouse, Reese. There's dirty business in the air."

Canby nodded. "Heard so, Cap. But what can I do?"

"You figure to do something, or you wouldn't have ridden in," countered Cap, his ragged white mustache bristling. "Just two men in this stretch of country that Antone and his tribe fully trust. You and Newt Dyas. Newt don't draw much water with some people I might name. You do. Antone will be glad to see you."

Canby spun a cigarette into shape.

"The old story of the lie and the double-cross again, maybe, Cap?"

"That's it," growled Cap. "Forty years I've put in in this country. I knew Arizona when it was a howlin' wilderness from one border to the other. I fought all through the Apache wars. I got a scar that still aches me, where an Apache arrow skidded across my ribs. But I never could bring myself to hate the Apache like some men did. They fought the only way they knew how for what they figured were their rights, same as anybody else would do who owned an ounce of salt. And this I know. The Apache was lied to and lied about. He was buncoed and swindled time an' again. Now, it looks like there's more of the same shaping up."

"Henry Joel says it was Sax Starke and Chelso De Lacca who were bringing the charges," observed Canby.

Cap Lovelock snorted. "Who else would it be? And the two of them are out to make fools of other men who should know better."

"What other men, Cap?"

"Bert Lanifee for one. Mason Garr for another. George Winter and Milt Parrall for two more. Which does surprise me. I thought Lanifee and Parrall were much too smart to be suckered.

Mason Garr, well, he's a tough monkey and a tough hater. George Winter is the sort to drift with the crowd. You know, Reese, I've heard it said that every man has his price, and I never agreed with that. But maybe, if the bait is big enough and rich enough—!" Cap broke off, shrugging.

"Bait like a share of Sentinel Basin grass, Cap?" prompted Canby.

"That's it!"

Reese Canby took a deep inhale from his cigarette, flipped the butt aside. A certain bleakness had deepened in him, leveling his lips, frosting up the clear gray of his eyes.

"Once," he said evenly, "I had just cause to throw a gun on Saxon Starke. Maybe I'll always regret that I didn't. Well, I'll look into things. Sandy, take care of the broncs."

He went up the street afoot, past Bob Stent's general store, past the Stag Head and the Desert House and all the other sun-bleached buildings of various sizes and meaning along this dusty way. On the porch of his hotel Billy Eustace sat in a battered old rocking chair, a mail sack at his feet. He scrubbed the sweat from his round bald head with a faded bandanna and swore softly.

"Damped hot day, Reese. But, hot or cold, some men lie easy."

Canby paused, met the hotel owner's bland blue eye.

“Don’t skitter around so, Billy. Come to the point.”

Billy Eustace took a swipe at a persistent fly, pursed his lips, and blew out a soft breath.

“There is not and never was any truth in Rupe Scudder or Jack Naile. They’re the two main witnesses. Was somebody to bust them two down, then Sax Starke wouldn’t have a leg to stand on.”

“That, friend Billy, is a thought,” agreed Canby. “Thanks.”

He went on to where the courthouse tilted its bare, two-storied blockiness high and unlovely in the sun. Across the parched earth in front of it a few cottonwoods drooped listlessly, and in the scanty shade of these squatted some dozen unmoving, taut, saturnine figures. Small men, cinder-dark from inherited eons of desert sun.

The younger wore their hair in twin braids pulled forward over either shoulder, their flat-brimmed hats perched high on their heads. But Antone, the old chief of these Mescalero Apaches, immobile in their midst, wore no hat, and his hair hung loose and straight, bound against his head with a cloth brow band. His eyes, jet beads in his wrinkled face, were fixed on Reese Canby, though he made no move and gave no sound.

Canby dropped on his heels beside the old chief and spoke quietly in the Mescalero tongue.

“The young men did not steal the cattle?”

The movement of Antone's head was barely perceptible, his spoken answer as thin and dry as the rustling of mesquite leaves.

"They did not steal."

Canby waited. He knew the way of the Apache. The old chief would say more in his own good time. He did. He told the story simply and without emphasis. Truth needed no embellishment.

Canby nodded toward the courthouse.

"You have spoken so in there?"

"The young men have. But the white man does not wish to believe."

Canby stood up. "Some white men do," he said quietly. "We'll see."

He headed for the courthouse door. A figure stepped into view around the corner of the building. Newt Dyas was of medium size, thinned and sweated to stringy whang leather by a lifetime under the desert sun. A bleached, neutral-colored man, still-faced, eyes puckered in a continual sun squint. His voice was dry, colorless.

"Hello, Reese. If you'd hit town sooner, you might have done some good. Late now, though. I've been listening under the courtroom window. The jury just went out."

"How do you figure it, Newt?" Canby asked.

Dyas shrugged. "When you're aimin' at a big steal yourself, it sometimes helps your case if you can make the other feller out a thief first."

An abrupt harshness roughened Canby's tone.

"It's so damned bare-faced. You'd think Judge Marland would see through the whole dirty business."

Newt Dyas swung his thin shoulders again in that faint, almost fatalistic shrug.

"Mebbe's got his suspicions and more'n likely has. But what can he do? The question of guilt is up to the jury. And it's Sax Starke's jury."

"All of it, Newt?"

"All but mebbe one. Oscar Heddon. A pretty fair man, Oscar. And he can be a damn stubborn one, as you know. Likewise, he's not afraid of Sax Starke. Oscar could hang this jury."

There came the rumble of movement along the hallway of the courthouse, the thump of boot heels, jangle of spurs, and the bursting growl of men's voices released from a period of more or less enforced silence.

Chelso De Lacca was the first to appear, then Mason Garr and Saxon Starke, side by side. After them came George Winter, Milt Parrall, and Bert Lanifee, the latter with his crutch and crippled leg. Following were several of the citizens of town and a scattering of riders, spur rowels chuffing. Tobacco sacks were switching back and forth, smokes being rolled.

Chelso De Lacca's heavy swart face held its usual shine of sweat, and his shirt, clinging tight to the lumpy round of his beefy shoulders, was dark and soggy where more of the same had damped through. His lips were heavy as he grinned, his teeth big and stained. His voice was moist and meaty.

"You're late, Canby. Missed all the fun. All over but the shoutin' now."

Reese Canby had never known any other feeling than a deep repulsion toward Chelso De Lacca. There was a ponderous grossness about the man, a loose effusiveness which fronted for something that peered out of eyes as secretive and soiled as pools of scummed water. He knew that De Lacca was taunting him right now. He looked the man up and down coldly.

"Our ideas of fun differ, Chelso. Never include me in your company. There's a sliminess about you that I like less and less."

Canby's voice was low-pitched, but it held a carrying note that cut through the casual talk of the emerging group. They quieted, and a thread of chilled tautness ran through the day's heat.

Saxon Starke swung forward, ranging up beside De Lacca.

"Canby, you got a rough tongue. Watch yourself!"

Reese Canby smiled only with his lips.

"Let him answer for himself. I'll get around to you next, Starke."

Chelso De Lacca laughed with a queer, husky moistness.

"Pay him no mind, Sax. He's been back in the

piñon country too long. It affects some that way. Me, I want a drink, and I'll buy. Come on!"

De Lacca moved away at his heavy rolling stride, drawing some of the more thirsty ones of the crowd with him.

Saxon Starke lingered. A well-set-up, bold-featured man, he was tall enough to look Reese Canby levelly in the eye. His hair was vigorous and tawny, inclined to curl.

A handsome man, thought Canby, and one you had to take apart, feature by feature, to realize that under his crisp mustache his lips were thin and ungenerous and that his eyes were of a blue that was marble hard and pale to coldness. Here, when aroused, was a man who could be vastly cruel. And one who would press home any advantage he felt was his at a given moment. Surrounded by friends, he seemed to feel that this was such a moment.

"What was the idea of rawhiding Chelso that way?" he demanded. "He met you pleasant enough, Canby."

The answer Starke got was as blunt as his question.

"He represents a part of something I don't like. And he oozes. There's slime on him. I wonder how you can stomach him as a partner, Starke, unless it happens to be that like appeals to like."

This was as harsh as a slap in the face. Sax Starke rocked forward on his toes, pale lightning in his eyes. But Mason Garr grabbed him and pulled him back, while Bert Lanifee swung expertly on his crutch to face Canby.

"Reese," rapped Lanifee angrily, "what the devil's the matter with you? You can't talk to a decent man that way. Sax would be justified if he—"

"Threw a gun on me, maybe," cut in Canby. "Well, now, Bert, don't worry about me, and don't anybody hold him back on my account."

Now it was Milt Parrall who swung in and grabbed Canby by the arm.

"You're way out of line, Reese. Cut it fine!"

George Winter came in on Canby from the other side, reaching out a placating hand which Canby brushed aside.

"You mean well, George," Canby told him. "But you're too close to my gun hand. Stay wide! Why don't you fellows leave this strictly up to Starke and me? If he wants it, he can have it."

This was definitely tossing more fuel on the flames, but it was in Reese Canby at the moment to keep the thing moving. This was the loosening up and boiling over of the cold, still anger that had been simmering deep within him ever since Henry Joel had stopped in at the summer cattle camp back in the Chevron Mountains with word of what was taking place here in Cassadora.

Mason Garr had help now. He nodded up several punchers who formed a loose ring around

Sax Starke and put on a pressure which started Starke moving off down the street toward the Desert House. The cold tension began to lift.

Milt Parrall, who had lost his cigarette, began rolling another while he spoke irritably.

"Sometimes, Reese, you're a trial to your best friends. Here you haven't been in town for months, and you show up with a chip on your shoulder and a burr under your tail. What the hell's got into you, man?"

Canby grinned bleakly, his eyes still following the tall figure of Saxon Starke.

"My best friends ought to know by this time that, whatever else my faults, being mealy-mouthed isn't one of them. I say what I think."

"All right. So you do. But do you have to be so damned blunt about it? Sax Starke is a proud man."

Canby spat deliberately.

"Proud about what? Being a thief, maybe?"

"Good Lord, Reese, not so loud!" protested Parrall. "That's fighting talk in any language."

"Maybe I mean it to be, Milt. And it's the truth. Sax Starke hadn't been in these parts three months before I found him feeding my beef to his crew. In my book, that makes him a thief."

"I know all about that," grunted Milt Parrall, still irritable. "It's an old story. But Sax claimed an honest mistake, and I believe him. He offered to pay you for the beef, didn't he?"

Reese Canby's lips twisted sardonically.

"That was only because he was caught at his dirty work. He put up that stall to fool the natives. But he wasn't fooling me then, and he's not now. Wish I could say the same for several others I know."

Milt Parrall spread his hands helplessly.

"I pass. When you get off on a tangent like this, there's no reasoning with you. Come on down to the Stag Head. I'll buy you a drink, and maybe that'll smooth your ruffled feathers."

Canby shook his head.

"Some other time. Right now, I got things to do. I'll be seeing you around. And Milt, next time don't step between Starke and me."

Milt Parrall stared at Canby for a long moment. Then he said, "I never saw you quite like this before, friend. I'm not promising a single damn thing."

Milt turned on his heel and walked away.

Reese Canby went over to where the Apaches were grouped, and he knew by the sharp glint in their glances that they had not missed a single word or inflection of tone that had taken place. There was something almost like the ghost of a smile touching the stern lips of Antone, the aged chief.

Canby talked with Antone for a good half-hour, after which the Apaches got their horses and left town in a group, heading east around the base of

Pahvant Rim and disappearing into the roll of country beyond.

Newt Dyas, coming up from nowhere, spoke in his slow, dry way.

"That was smart, Reese, getting Antone and his crowd out of town. There's more dynamite in this thing than a lot of folks realize. The old, wild days of insurrection are long gone, but the fires of pride and independence and the will to fight if he has to still burn in the Apache. If they give Antone enough cause, he's liable to raise hell and put a chunk under it."

"And that," nodded Canby, gravely thoughtful, "is what we've got to head off at all costs, Newt." The bright chill that had frosted his eyes had now begun to fade, leaving in its place a sober concern. "Where's Jack Naile and Rupe Scudder?"

Newt Dyas's head gave a faint upward swing, like an old hound that had sniffed an unexpected trail.

"What about Naile and Scudder, Reese?"

"Star witnesses, ain't they?"

"That's right. Mike Partman's riding herd on them. I wouldn't be surprised if Partman didn't have his orders from Sax Starke."

"Or me," nodded Canby. "Starke seems to have a genius for corrupting everything he touches. Do me a favor, Newt. Stick around the courthouse and let me know when the jury makes up its mind. You'll find me at Bob Stent's store or over at Billy Eustace's hotel. And, Newt, have a bronc ready where you can grab it at notice."

Newt Dyas gnawed the end off of a twist of tobacco, rolled it in one gaunt, leathery cheek, his eyes squinting a little tighter.

"We'll have trouble, Reese—getting Naile and Scudder away from Partman."

"Maybe. But if the verdict comes in as guilty, Partman will lose interest in them in a hurry. Then it will be our turn."

"Dangerous stuff, boy," murmured Dyas.

Canby shrugged. "If all trails were smooth, what would be the fun of riding them?"

"You got something there," admitted Newt Dyas with a faint dry smile. "I'll be around."

Canby went on down to Bob Stent's store, stopped just short of the wide, warmly shadowed door, reaching for his hat.

"Hello, Chris," he said. "This makes the ride in from the Chevrons plenty worthwhile."

Christine Lanifee had just stepped from the store door, and now she looked him over gravely, a faint frown touching the brown smoothness of her face.

"I'm not so sure of that, Reese," she answered. "I hear there was an argument down at the courthouse, and that you started it. Just who do you consider to be your real friends, anyhow?"

Her slimness made her appear taller than she

really was. Her shoulders were fine and erect, and when she moved a step or two farther from the doorway, there was a smooth, free grace to her stride. A reaching shaft of sunlight brought out the auburn sheen in her hair, and the clear hazel of her eyes seemed gold-flecked as she squinted a trifle against the reflected glare of the dust-white street.

"I always have loved that," drawled Canby softly.

Her head swung quickly. "Loved what?"

"The way you wrinkle your nose when you squint against the sun. Reminds me of the freckle-faced little girl who used to play with me and Ponco and Dobe and the rest of the Apache kids over on the reservation while her pa was unloading supplies from his freight wagon."

"Then," she said crisply, "it should also remind you that that little girl's father was killed by the very Apaches he freighted food to. Maybe you've forgotten that, Reese. I haven't and I never will."

"By Apaches, Chris—but not the same Apaches. It was a Chiricahua war party that ambushed your father's wagon train. No Mescalero would ever have harmed him."

"They're all Apaches," said the girl coldly.

"That's dangerous thinking, Chris," warned Canby soberly. "There was fault on both sides in that war, and both sides lost good men. War is always like that. And you wouldn't want to see another outbreak come, would you?"

"That's a silly question. Of course I wouldn't!"

"Don't bet against it if certain schemers have their way. That's what the argument was about over at the courthouse. I was giving my opinion of certain men who, if they have their way, will start some wicked trouble in these parts."

He watched the softness of her chin harden to stubborn lines. This girl had strong convictions.

"You've never liked Saxon Starke or Chelso De Lacca," she said, "so your judgment of them is bound to be colored by your personal feelings."

"Perhaps," Canby conceded. "Yet it is also colored by my feelings toward other people. I grew up with Ponco and Dobe. After my father died, old Antone was the kindest man in the world to me. He's an honorable old man, Antone is. He wouldn't lie to save his own life—literally. He gave me his word that Ponco and Dobe never stole any cattle. I believe him. If those two Apache boys are sent over the road for something they did not do, this country is going to see trouble. Somebody is lying, Chris—and it's not the Apaches."

There was no break in her stubborn mood.

"I believe my own brother and stand on his judgment. Bert is convinced."

"Sax Starke," said Canby, a hint of dry bitterness in his tone, "is a smooth talker. Bert Lanifee isn't the only one Starke is fooling."

He saw her eyes flash. "Then you consider Bert a fool?"

The eager pleasure that had been in Reese Canby's eyes since first sight of her faded to a weary bleakness. But he kept his tone gentle.

"I didn't say that, Chris. And I don't want to argue with you. You know that. For you've always blinded my eye, even back in the days when you were that freckle-faced little girl I just spoke of. But Chris, right is right and wrong is wrong. There is no halfway measure in a thing of this sort. Your brother Bert, among others, is being taken in by Sax Starke and Chelso De Lacca."

He saw the anger building up in her, but it struck him that there was a certain irritability in that anger, as though she were less sure of herself than she seemed, as though her anger were directed as much at herself as at him. He was seeking words to mend this mood when boot heels struck hard on the end of the store porch, and Mason Garr's voice rang out, with all the man's usual harsh bluntness.

"Want to *habla* with you, Canby. Sorry to break into your chat, Chris, but Canby here needs some telling to, and I've elected myself to the chore."

Chris Lanifee hesitated, biting a soft underlip,

then she said, “It’s all right, Mr. Garr. I was just about to leave.”

She moved away, her shoulders uncompromisingly straight, her shining head high.

Reese Canby watched her go, paying Mason Garr no attention until he felt the man’s presence right at his shoulder. Then he spoke, his voice low and brittle.

“If you ever move in on me again, Mason, at such a time and with that kind of a tone, I’ll knock your words right back down your throat. Now, damn you, what do you want?”

Chapter II
DESERT JUDGMENT

Mason Garr was stocky, with a blunt jaw and a ruggedly hard, deeply weathered face. By habit, his manner was as blunt as his jaw, and his courage beyond question. Yet he moved back a step as Reese Canby spun to face him.

"All right," snapped Canby again. "What do you want? Trouble, maybe? Why not let Sax Starke skin his own cats?"

Rough and tough as he was, Mason Garr knew when to heed the danger signals. They were flying now.

"Say I did come at you wrong and at a poor time," he admitted gruffly. "But I know you, and I know Sax Starke. And I know it won't be good for this country if you two come to a smoke rolling. For some damn reason, your roach is up, and you're ready to snap. I'm here to try to smooth things out."

Some of the hard and vibrant edge went out of Reese Canby. He even managed a mirthless grin.

"You smooth things with a heavy hand, man. But say your piece."

"I'm trying to figure you," said Mason Garr.

"You hit town, you walk up the street with wider steps than I've ever seen you use before. You go out of your way to throw the rawhide at Chelso De Lacca and Sax Starke. You act like you'd been feeding on raw meat. Why?"

"Put it down that I don't like the smell of a dirty deal being pulled against old and good friends of mine," answered Canby curtly. "Particularly when it's being engineered by a couple of men I wouldn't trust as far as I can spit. The thing that really shakes me up is the following those two liars have acquired. There's a lot of rough edges to you, Mason, which make you a hard man to like. But I've always figured you as square and nobody's fool. Now, as I see it, you're either a fool or not as square as I thought you were."

Here was talk as blunt as any Mason Garr had ever put out himself. A tide of color flickered across the rough-edged cattleman's face.

"I've never been a damned hypocrite," he growled. "I never did believe that the government had any right to set aside Sentinel Basin for the exclusive use of Apache cattle. I've made myself plain on that plenty of times. And on other things too. Such as not likin' Apaches, which I never did and never will. I don't trust 'em, and I wouldn't take the word of one of them on a stack of Bibles."

Canby eyed Mason Garr keenly.

"You really believe that, don't you? You really

believe that Ponco and Dobe did steal some Starke and De Lacca cows—or try to?"

"Of course I do!" asserted Garr explosively. "And I figure it ain't the first time. The Apache has got the slickest cattle-stealing setup in the world. You know how they handle their herd—a tribal affair, with every buck in the tribe owning a divvy and a brand. Why, even the Apache kids, soon as they're old enough, get a brand they can slap on a calf or two."

Canby nodded. "That's correct. But what's wrong with such an arrangement? Everybody benefits."

"Everybody but the man who has a herd of his own running anywhere near Sentinel Basin," said Garr. "You know how Apache brands are. Nobody but an Apache can figure them out. You can take any legitimate brand you want to name, blot it some damn crazy way, and call it an Apache brand. You throw that critter into Sentinel Basin, mix it up with a jag of other cattle, all wearing a tangle of other Apache brands. Who in hell is going to find the critter and prove ownership? Not you or me or anybody else."

Mason Garr made a hard gesture with a clenched fist, then went on.

"By the time the Apache gets ready to sell off some stuff, show me a buyer who pays a damn bit of attention to the brands. There are so many different ones that the buyer would go crazy trying to figure them out. So he buys the cattle by lot and lets it go at that. Hell, man! Give me the same chance the Apache has, and I'll grow hog rich in five years off other people's cattle."

Canby spun a cigarette into shape.

"All these things you speak of could be done," he admitted. "But that doesn't prove they are being done. You got a right to your opinion, and I have to mine, Mason. I don't believe Antone and his people are cow thieves. I remember too many fine things about them during the ten years my father spent as Indian agent on the reservation."

"And me," rapped Garr, "I remember a few things about the Apache myself. I remember the wars. I remember burying a brother of mine after the Apache got through with him. Yeah, I'll remember that all my life."

"Then," murmured Canby, "you no doubt remember the massacre on Blood Creek. What named that creek, Mason? Apache blood did. There was that little settlement of Mescaleros, tilling their fields, guarding their flocks, minding their own business, and harming no one. After the treacherous massacre, only a handful were left. Most of the casualties were squaws and papooses. And not six months after the massacre, the land those unfortunate Mescaleros had held ended up in possession of certain white men who led the massacre and who had wanted that land all the time. While you're remembering, Mason, you might recall that."

Garr again swung his fist in that hard, characteristic gesture.

"This ain't gettin' us nowhere. We could stand here and argue all day. I'll say what I came to say, then get about my business."

"And what did you come to say?" Reese Canby's voice was very quiet.

"Why, for you to lay off Sax Starke and Chelso De Lacca." All of Mason Garr's blunt roughness was back now. "Lay off 'em, because there's several of us who see eye to eye with them in this thing and who stand to back their hands all the way. Get that, Canby—all the way!"

Reese Canby was silent for some little time, hands on his hips, his glance sweeping up and down the street with a narrowing bleakness. Abruptly, he nodded, as though he had irrevocably made up his mind on something. He spoke crisply.

"Fair enough. That's your say. Here's mine. I say that the same damned greed that's been running in Starke and De Lacca is now running in you and others. You've gone blind to realities, thinking about Sentinel Basin grass. You're crawling right down to the level of Starke and De Lacca, and, mister, that's pretty damned low. So now I tell you this. I lay my own trail. Should it lead me to Starke and De Lacca, don't you or anybody else try to cut it. You can pass that word along. That's how it will be, Mason."

Mason Garr said not another word. He turned and tramped away in that solid-heeled manner of his. Canby watched him go, a shadow of regret in his eyes, for he had always known a certain liking for Mason Garr.

The Red Mountain stage rumbled into town, coming in from the east, already gray with the dust it had picked up in the ten miles it had covered since leaving Reservation. It puffed up in front of the hotel with a squeal of brakes and jangle of harness.

Billy Eustace hoisted himself out of his chair, handed up the mail sack to the driver, and stood talking for a moment. Reese Canby took a final drag from his cigarette, spun the butt into the street, and turned into Bob Stent's store. The stage rocked into movement again, heading west out of town and, as distance took it over, seemed to float in its accompanying cloud of dust.

The furious sun was gone, and the first illusory coolness of shadow stole across the world. The desert turned to a sea of swimming purple and powder blue, and the Pahvant Rim became a wall of steadily darkening maroon.

In the Stent living quarters out back of the store, Reese Canby and Sandy Foss sprawled in the unaccustomed ease of chairs and talked in low tones, cautious eyes watching the kitchen door across this pleasant, homey room, a door letting out the savory odors of cooking food. A moment later, that door framed the comely picture of Mary Stent.

In the lamplight, she reflected a wholesome sturdiness, with blue-black hair, snapping dark eyes, and a generous, flushed face. There was an unquenchable merriness and cheer in this girl and a quick, penetrating wit.

"What are you two ragamuffins mumbling and whispering about?" she demanded. "What's all the mystery?"

Reese Canby grinned.

"The mystery is you, Mary. We can't figure how your father has managed to hang on to you for so long, what with all the lonesome young saddle pounders roaming these parts. Now you take Sandy here. I know that if you'd just say the word, Sandy would—"

"You lay off Sandy Foss," interrupted that badgered and red-faced individual. "Don't you believe a word he says, Mary. He can be the lyin'est jigger—!" Sandy floundered to a stop, all thumbs and feet and embarrassed indignation.

Mary laughed softly.

"I take no stock in his blarney, Sandy. And I'll always be true to you."

Reese Canby's grin became a chuckle, while Sandy's confusion grew.

Bob Stent, who had been out front waiting on

a late customer, came in hungry and rubbing his hands.

"Supper's late, I bet, what with you three making small talk."

"That's where you're wrong, Father dear," retorted Mary. "Supper is ready and waiting on you."

They gathered about the table, with its covering of red-and-white checked cloth. Bob Stent was a cheerful, open-handed man, without an enemy in the world. But he was long-headed, and now, as he pulled up a chair, he looked across at Reese Canby with some gravity.

"Things are in the air that I don't like, Reese. What are they going to lead to?"

"Trouble, maybe, unless enough public opinion can be brought against Sax Starke and Chelso De Lacca to make them take a different trail than the one they're on now."

"That," mused Bob Stent, "may take some doing. If it was De Lacca alone, it might not be too difficult. But Sax Starke is a stubborn, willful man."

"You're too kind, Bob," observed Canby dryly. "You leave the picture half-painted, with only the best colors showing. In my book, there's a lot to be said about Sax Starke, and none of it good."

"You can," put in Mary Stent unexpectedly, "apply the same to Chelso De Lacca, Reese. He gives me the creeps."

Bob Stent looked at his daughter in some surprise. “As a rule, you’ve no criticism against anyone, Mary. What have you got against Chelso?”

Mary colored slightly. “Put it that I simply can’t stand sight of the man.”

Bob Stent attacked his steak a trifle fiercely.

“I try and see the best side of a man. The word is around that Starke and De Lacca have eyes on Sentinel Basin. That’s hard to believe. But taking it as true, do you think that would mean a fight by Antone, Reese?”

“No doubt of it.” Canby nodded. “And who could blame him? Sax Starke knows it, too, and ten to one is gambling on it. There’s nothing he’d like better than to see Antone pick up the rifle again. He knows that old memories and hatreds still linger with a lot of people. He knows that in a showdown, the Apaches wouldn’t stand a chance. No matter how right Antone might be, in the public eye, he’d be all wrong. Starke knows that. He knows, too, that if things got too bad and out of hand, the troops would move in once more. So, as I see it, Starke is out to put the onus on Antone and his people from any possible angle, to make them scapegoats. He wants to see them pushed back to the old reservation status, which would leave Sentinel Basin open for him to move into.”

Bob Stent, stubbornly fair, said, “That’s a pretty

heavy indictment of the man, Reese. I know that you and Sax never did get along. I wonder how much of your angle is based on personal dislike?"

Canby shrugged. "Open your eyes wide, Bob, and take a good look in all directions. Then open your mind. I'll rest on the answer you find. Didn't you just admit there were things in the air you didn't like?"

"I did, and there are. Yet there are several good men more or less inclined to believe as Starke does and to follow his lead. I'm referring to Bert Lanifee, Mason Garr, Milt Parrall, and George Winter. If you damn Starke and De Lacca in this thing, Reese, you must damn those others too."

"That," admitted Canby quietly, "is the part that hurts. Those men are friends of mine—or were." His tone went slightly bitter. "I wish I knew whether they're foolishly blind or willfully so."

"Let's talk of something else," said Mary Stent. "I didn't plan this as a gloomy event, but as a festive occasion to welcome a pair of shaggy timber wolves back into the circle of civilized society. I even baked a pie in celebration. Suppose, for a change, we talk about us. When are you going back to the Chevrons, Reese?"

"Depends," Canby answered, a smile driving some of the grimness from his lips. "If I could board here regular, I'd never go back. I'd set out to beat Sandy's time. Maybe I won't go back at all this year. The season is running along. The boys I left up there can take care of the cattle until first snow flies without me cluttering up the scenery. But I may send Sandy back. With him out of the way, maybe you and I could make moon talk."

Mary dimpled. "Shame on you, Reese Canby. What would Chris Lanifee say if she heard you talking so?"

"Ha!" exclaimed Sandy Foss in high satisfaction. "Good girl, Mary! Go ahead, lather him some more."

Canby threw up both hands in mock protest.

"You win, Mary. I quit. But how's chances for a look at that pie?"

They had finished eating and were lingering over a final cup of coffee when a knock sounded at the rear kitchen door. Canby got to his feet.

"Let me answer that."

He opened the door and stepped through into the night. Newt Dyas was just a shadow, and his voice whisper-soft.

"Jury's comin' in, Reese. They must have talked down Oscar Heddon. It takes longer than just a few hours of wranglin' to declare a hung jury. I'm afraid it's goin' to be—guilty."

"I figured it would be," murmured Canby. "Wait here, Newt."

He opened the door and stepped back into the Stent kitchen. He looked at Sandy Foss.

"All right, kid. You know what to do. Mary—Bob, thanks for everything."

Sandy picked up his hat and was heading for the door when Mary caught at him, vague alarm forming in her eyes.

"Sandy! What is it?"

The boyishness faded from Sandy's face, leaving him all man. He patted her hand gently.

"Nothing for you to worry about, Mary. Just a little idea Reese and I cooked up. I'll be underfoot again as usual in a day or two."

Sandy ducked out of the door and headed for the livery barn. Mary Stent looked at Reese Canby very directly.

"He's just a boy, Reese. Don't lead him into anything."

"I think a lot of my right arm, but not half so much of it as I do of Sandy," reassured Canby. "He'll be all right, Mary. That's a promise."

"Has this got to be so mysterious, Reese?" asked Bob Stent. "What's it all about?"

"The jury's coming in, and it looks like a guilty verdict. And that's bad, Bob. Somebody has got to try to hold the lid on. I figure to do the best I can."

Canby stepped out, closed the door, and followed Newt Dyas away into the night.

There were lights in the courthouse and a murmur along the street, the stir of movement. From the Desert House, a dark blur of men moved toward the courthouse, men going to hear the verdict read and sentence pronounced.

Chelso De Lacca's heavy laugh rang out, confident of the result. Saxon Starke strode at the head of the crowd, a tall and dominant figure. From the shadows, Reese Canby and Newt Dyas watched, their eyes following Starke.

"The emperor complex, Newt," murmured Canby. "Alone, it's bad enough. Mix it with crooked scheming, and it can be poison."

"It's the fools who puzzle me," said Newt. "Them who are following him. Lanifee, Garr—the others. Damn fools or greedy ones. I never did put too much stock in human nature. This leaves me with less than before."

"Ordinarily," mused Canby, "if the accused were white men, a case like this wouldn't excite more than passing interest. A crowd certainly wouldn't pass up food and drink just to get the result firsthand. But this case is dynamite, and down deep even the dumbest realize it. Yet they trail along, letting Starke call the cards. We're liable to be damned unpopular around here, Newt."

"Reckon I can stand up to it," said Newt dryly.

"We've got to outguess Naile and Scudder," Canby reasoned. "While Mike Partman's had them in tow, they've left their broncs at the livery barn. Once Partman lets them go, they'll head for their horses sooner or later. That's when we'll move in."

"How about Pokey Carter?" asked Newt.

Canby grinned bleakly into the night.

"Pokey's a good friend of mine and can lie like a house afire when the occasion warrants. Don't worry about Pokey."

They built cigarettes and crouched there, prepared to wait this thing out. It shouldn't take too long. Judge Marland was noted for the speed with which he could close out a case once the arguing was all done, the verdict in, and the hour growing late.

"Better get over there, Newt," decided Canby. "Stick around long enough to hear the sentence."

Newt Dyas disappeared soundlessly, and Reese Canby was alone with his thoughts. He knew that what he had in mind was a long and somewhat risky chance. There was no guarantee that he could force Jack Naile or Rupe Scudder to talk. But maybe, if he put enough pressure on and played one against the other, he could break one of them down. Long chance or not, it was the only one open to him.

As silently as he had gone, Newt Dyas returned.

"Guilty," he said laconically. "And a year in Yuma. If Judge Marland had made it any less, he'd have turned Ponco and Dobe loose. I'd say that the judge is one man Sax Starke ain't foolin'."

Canby stood up, stretched. "Which leaves things strictly up to us. Let's get over to the stable. The party will be breaking up."

This was true. Men were already beginning to stream from the courthouse. Canby and Newt Dyas followed thick street shadows until they reached the livery barn, where they found Sandy Foss in earnest argument with Pokey Carter. Pokey was squatted on the edge of the bunk in his saddle-and-harness room, his shriveled, whiskey face gnome-like in the feeble lantern glow.

"What kind of fiddle-dee-dee are you up to, Reese Canby?" he demanded fretfully. "Here's this Sandy Foss arguin' ten to a dozen, tryin' to get me to go off and drown myself. But you ain't foolin' me. You jiggers are up to somethin'."

Canby dropped a dollar in Pokey's ancient paw.

"Go up to the Desert House and treat yourself to a couple, Pokey. Stay there until Sax Starke and Chelso De Lacca leave. If anybody asks you any questions, you don't know a thing, and you haven't seen a thing. As a favor to me, Pokey."

Some of Pokey's fretfulness vanished.

"Well, as long as you put it that way, Reese. But don't you muss things up."

Canby's grin was hard. "Anything we muss up won't belong to you, Pokey."

The little stable owner shuffled out.

"Our broncs are saddled and ready, Reese," said Sandy. "But Pokey wouldn't let me touch

Naile's and Scudder's. He was a stubborn little cuss until you dropped that dollar in his hand. Newt coming with us?"

"Coming along," Newt said briefly. "We better put out this light."

They doused the lantern and went out to the cavernous front door of the stable. At this end of the street, the night lay deeply dark, all the glow of the town farther west.

"Guilty and a year in Yuma," Canby told Sandy. "It could have been worse."

"Guilty, and five minutes in Mike Partman's lockup would have been too much," observed Sandy sagely. "It's the principle of the thing that'll set Antone off. I sure hope we draw some luck in this little soiree."

Again, they had to wait this thing out. Jack Naile and Rupe Scudder would be sure to stop in at the Desert House or the Stag Head for a couple of drinks. There was no telling when they'd come after their horses. Reese Canby's fervent wish was that they come alone.

Newt Dyas said, "I'll go locate their broncs and slap some saddles on, for once we get them two collared, it'll pay to move fast. Sax Starke may be crooked as a snake in a wagon track, but he's also shrewd enough to put two and two together and come up with the right answer. Once Naile and Scudder turn up missing, and with us nowhere in town, Starke will be sure to figure the right answer. Then he and De Lacca and their crowd will do some wide and fast ridin'. It could go rough with us if we happen to get in the way."

Newt drifted off, back into the blackness of the stable.

"That guy is half ghost," murmured Sandy Foss. "You don't hear him go; you don't hear him come. Most of the time, you don't see him, either. I'm sure glad he's not packing a blood grudge against me."

The night was cooling. A little wind that had finally managed to fight back the lingering updraft of the desert was flowing down over Pahvant Rim, and the breath of it was all of distance and sweet emptiness. An early coyote, liking the wind's flavor, perched on the rim and yapped at the stars, a sound small and remote against the vast spread of the night.

Sandy Foss jumped a foot when Newt Dyas settled noiselessly down beside him. Dry humor threaded Newt's tone.

"You got to learn to listen with the back of your neck, kid."

"That don't make sense," grumbled Sandy.

"It does when you learn the knack. And while we're listenin', who's comin' down street?"

"It could be the ones we want," murmured Canby.

It was. There was the shuffle of spurred boots,

then Jack Naile's droning, nasal voice, and finally, words from Rupe Scudder, heavy and clumsy as the man himself.

"Just why Sax should want us to scatter out of town so quick I can't figure," complained Scudder. "What the hell! It's all over, ain't it? Yet Sax allows just two drinks and then orders us back to headquarters. Just two drinks—and I was set to celebrate a little." Scudder's words drifted off into a dour curse.

Reese Canby, Sandy Foss, and Newt Dyas were on their feet now, drawn a trifle back into the blackness of the stable, just inside the door and to one side.

"I'll take the one in the lead," breathed Canby.

Jack Naile, always venomous of temper, cursed bitterly when faced with the blackness of the inner stable.

"That damn Pokey Carter, tellin' us to get our own broncs, with him lappin' up a few at the Desert House! How we gonna locate our gear in this black hole? I got a notion to—"

Naile's complaint broke off abruptly as Reese Canby, measuring distance and direction by sound alone, drew his gun, moved out, and swung the barrel of the weapon in a short, chopping arc. He felt the high crown of Naile's hat give under the weight of the gun and some of the impact take effect on the rider's head. But the blow was not so solid as it could have been, and Naile was only half-stunned as he stumbled to one side but did not go down.

Canby drove for him again, crashed into him, upset him completely, then fell over and past him. Underfoot was a thick pad of broken straw and other refuse, muffling their fall. Canby knew that Naile would be going for his gun and knew also that if Naile should get off a shot, even though it hit nothing, it would be an alarm that could upset the whole plan. So Canby came whirling desperately back, smashing out twice more with his gun barrel. The second try counted. The gun landed fully solid this time, and Naile went limp.

Behind him, Canby heard Newt Dyas's thin, dry drawl.

"Save your hustle, Sandy—Scudder's quiet. You all right, Reese?"

"All right. Bring up their broncs, Newt."

They tied Naile and Scudder across the saddles, went out the back way, where Sandy had Canby's and his own horse saddled and waiting.

Newt Dyas asked, "Where away, Reese?"

"Monument Rock is where Antone will be."

"Good! My horse is up by the courthouse. I'll pick you up."

Reese Canby led Naile's horse, Sandy led Scudder's. They circled beyond town, crossed the stage road, and drove straight south into the desert. The lights of Cassadora grew distant, the dark bulk of Pahvant Rim slowly receding against the stars. Within a mile, Newt Dyas caught up with them.

"All quiet back in town when I left," he reported.

The desert was deceptive. To the casual glance, it seemed flat, but there were long, sweeping rolls to it, with crests and hollows. They put a crest behind them that barred the fading lights of town completely. Now there was only emptiness and silence and star-touched earth.

Scudder and Naile began getting their senses back, and their muffled cursing was steady and painful.

The miles drifted back, and in time the desert thrust a humpbacked shadow against the stars. Close in the shadow grew blackly solid and showed a jagged, broken top. Monument Rock.

Reese Canby led a way around to the south side of it, reined in, and dismounted. While he and Sandy Foss untied and pulled Jack Naile and Rupe Scudder from their jolting, highly uncomfortable cross-saddle positions, Newt Dyas rustled up an armful of dry sage and built a small fire.

"Now," Canby told the prisoners grimly, "we'll go after some fresh testimony—this time the truth. And it had better be the truth!"

In the flicker of the meager firelight, Jack Naile's tight, pointed features were hard and snarling. This fellow was tough, and Canby doubted whether he could break him down. Rupe Scudder offered a better chance, for he was ponderous and slow-witted, not too sure of himself when at a disadvantage. He crouched beside Naile at the fire, rubbing his thick wrists where the ropes had chafed, staring with bloodshot eyes at the guns Reese Canby and Sandy Foss held openly.

Jack Naile was shrewd enough to see what was ahead.

"Don't tell 'em a damned thing, Rupe," he warned harshly. "They ain't got anything on us."

"Of that we'll see," said Canby bleakly. "Let's take a look at the proposition. On your testimony in Judge Marland's court, two Apache boys have just had a year in Yuma thrown at them on the charge of attempted cattle stealing. Your story was that the pair of you caught Ponco and Dobe driving some thirty head of Starke and De Lacca cows into Sentinel Basin. You say that when you surprised them, Ponco and Dobe hightailed, so that you were able to bunch the cows and get them out of the basin again. Right?"

Jack Naile spat and cursed. Rupe Scudder started to nod, caught himself, and said nothing.

"As always, there's another side to the story," went on Canby. "Ponco and Dobe claim they stumbled across that jag of Tepee cattle drifting down into the basin from Skeleton Wash. They bunched the stock and were heading them back when you two showed up. Ponco and Dobe didn't run. They told you what happened and turned the cattle over to you. That's the real story, and the one I believe."

"Whoever knew an Apache to tell the truth?" grunted Rupe Scudder sourly. "Only a damn fool would take the word of an Apache."

Jack Naile whirled on his companion. "Damn you, Rupe," he snarled, "I told you to keep your mouth shut. Don't answer a question, don't say a word!"

Reese Canby smiled thinly.

"Wouldn't be afraid, would you, Naile, that if Scudder got to arguing, he might let out some of the real truth? If you weren't a pair of liars, you wouldn't be afraid to talk."

Naile's eyes reflected a hard glitter in the firelight.

"You've moved into something you'll live to be damn sorry about, Canby. That takes in Foss and Dyas, too. I don't take this sort of thing lyin' down, not from you or anybody else. That you'll see!"

Canby shrugged.

"Even if I was scared, which I'm not, I'd still have to go along with this thing, Naile. So let's look at a few more details. Ponco and Dobe were smart enough to realize it was hardly likely that a bunch of cows that size would drift into Sentinel

Basin on their own. So after you two pulled out, Ponco and Dobe backtracked along Skeleton Wash. They found that the cattle had definitely been bunched on Starke and De Lacca's Stony Flat range, then brought in past the Brothers, and headed down Skeleton Wash—by two riders. Now you wouldn't have any idea who those two riders could have been, would you, Rupe?"

Scudder held his surly silence, just crouching there, glowering at the flames.

"All right," went on Canby. "I already know the answer to that. Dobe and Ponco found it out. They checked the tracks of the horses that bunched and started the cows along Skeleton Wash. Then they checked the tracks of the broncs you two were up on when they turned the cattle back to you. The tracks of both places matched very nicely. Sandy, bring Rupe Scudder's horse over here by the fire. That's it. Pretty good bronc this, eh, Rupe? Favorite of yours. You ride it a lot. But this near front hoof, it toes in a little. You should have remembered that before you set out on that Sentinel Basin deal. For if there's anything in the world you can't fool an Apache on, it's the earth and the signs men and horses leave on it."

Scudder squirmed slightly. "Plenty of broncs pack a toed-in hoof," he blurted. "Don't mean a thing."

Jack Naile rose half up, glaring at Scudder and

starting his venomous cursing again. Sandy Foss waggled his gun.

"Sit down, Naile—and stay down! Keep your gab to yourself. This little chat is between Reese and Scudder."

Canby kept his full concentration boring at Rupe Scudder, for he could see the shine of sweat begin to slime Scudder's face.

"That's right, Rupe, plenty of broncs do toe in with a hoof. But not all the same amount or the same way or with the same hoof. There's always a mite of difference that marks each one. Yeah, you were careless, you and Naile. So it shapes up that you two drove those cows into Sentinel Basin, hung around until some of the Apache riders discovered them and started to move them. When Dobe and Ponco did, you set up the yell of cattle stealing. Pretty barefaced and raw, Rupe. But Sax Starke and Chelso De Lacca figured they'd have enough public opinion backing them, based on old hatreds, to make such a thin charge stand up."

Jack Naile swung his narrow head.

"You been readin' too many fairy stories, Canby. How long did it take you to think up all that hogwash?"

"I didn't have to think up anything," rapped Canby. "Antone gave me the story. Now you two are going to corroborate it, the hard way if necessary."

Naile spat into the flames. "I don't scare worth a damn."

"Seems like he just brought us out here to talk us to death, eh, Jack?" mumbled Rupe Scudder, in a heavy attempt at humor.

"Oh, I don't intend to rough you up, personally," said Canby easily. "I'll leave that to Antone and some of his braves. The Apache always did have ways and means of making even the most stubborn man talk."

Rupe Scudder shifted uneasily. For a moment, Jack Naile was very still. Then he spoke droningly.

"You wouldn't dare, Canby. You couldn't get away with it. You'd be run out of the country if you were lucky. Otherwise, you'd stay here forever, but you wouldn't be livin'."

"I'll dare plenty to keep an old-time outbreak from exploding again," said Canby, suddenly very grim. "The lives and feelings of you two whelps would be nothing against the hell and misery another Apache outbreak would bring to a lot of good people—on both sides. As for getting away with it, well, do you think Starke or De Lacca have the slightest idea where you are right now? And if you disappear completely, who's to guess how or where? It's a big country, plenty big enough to hide your bones."

Rupe Scudder cleared his throat thickly.

"Them two bucks only got a year in Yuma Penitentiary. A year ain't so long."

"It's a lifetime when the charge is false. I can see just two ways to keep Antone and his tribe from jumping the gun again. One is for you jingos to tell the real truth of this thing to Judge Marland, which will mean the immediate release of Ponco and Dobe from custody. The other is to turn you over to Antone and let him take payment in his own way—an eye for an eye. The Apache is quite willing to live by the white man's law as long as it represents true justice. But when it doesn't, then they make their own law. It's liable to be pretty rough on you two. Think it over. I mean business, and the choice is strictly up to you."

"We've told our story," snarled Jack Naile. "We'll stick by it. Don't let him scare you, Rupe. He's bluffing."

"Your last word?" demanded Canby.

Naile did not answer, and Scudder held silent, too, taking his cue from his companion.

"All right," said Reese Canby, "you've asked for it."

He turned to face the outer dark, cupped his hands about his mouth, and sent the hoot of an owl drifting in clear hollowness across the night. Almost immediately, an answer came back.

Canby turned back to the fire and rolled a smoke with steady hands.

Rupe Scudder and Jack Naile had heard that

answering owl hoot. Naile's head was tipped, his hard eyes probing the dark. Scudder was staring out, too, the sweep of a nervous tongue moistening his lips. The stir of approaching steps was like a faint wind rustle. Then Antone and half a dozen of his braves moved into the thin outer edge of the firelight.

Rupe Scudder lunged half erect, then dropped back, an oath breaking from him in a muffled cry. Jack Naile seemed to draw within himself, tight and trapped and venomous. Then he surged upright, leaping for his horse. Sandy Foss tripped him and dropped him. Newt Dyas moved in to help.

"You see," said Canby to Scudder, "for all his big talk, Naile was ready to cut and run for it and leave you to face the music alone."

Rupe Scudder swung his head back and forth, the shine of fear growing in his eyes. The first heavy, slow truculence was running out of him. There was little imagination in Rupe Scudder, but what there was of it was working overtime now. He had not fought in any of the Apache wars, but he'd heard plenty of talk by old-timers of what the Apaches could do to a man once they set their minds to it. He licked his lips again and spoke thickly.

"What do I get if I talk to Judge Marland, Canby?"

"Whatever you get won't be a tenth as much as

you'll get if you don't." Canby nodded toward the silent waiting Apaches.

Jack Naile, struggling uselessly in the grip of Sandy Foss and Newt Dyas, cursed wildly.

"Rupe! Keep your damn mouth shut!"

Rupe Scudder did not seem to hear. He kept staring across the fading fire at Antone and his braves. His was a one-track mind. It ran in this groove or that. Now it was seeing the Apache at work on him. The greasy sweat shine on his face grew.

"All right," he croaked. "Take me to Judge Marland!"

Chapter III
LYING WITNESS

Judge Hobart Marland was a thin, waspy man with a shock of snow-white hair and an imperial of the same color. Reese Canby's insistent knock got the judge out of bed, and he answered the door in a robe and tattered slippers. He held a lamp high, and the light of it reflected the snapping impatience in his eyes.

"Is anything so important it couldn't have waited until morning?" he demanded testily.

"I'll let you decide that, Judge, after five minutes of your time," answered Canby. "All right, Scudder—inside!"

As Canby pushed Rupe Scudder through the door ahead of him, Judge Marland eyed Scudder in open distaste.

"I think little of your company, Canby. I believe this fellow to be a lying scoundrel. If I ever listened to perjured testimony in my life, I listened to it from him and that fellow Naile. But I couldn't prove it, and the jury chose to believe them."

"That's just why I'm getting you out of bed at this time of night, Judge," said Canby. "Scudder here is ready to admit he made some serious mistakes in his testimony. In case he tries to go stubborn on us, I want your word for it that I can take him out of here just as I brought him in, with no questions asked, now or later."

As he spoke, Canby faced Judge Marland squarely, with narrowed meaning in his eyes. A glint of understanding came back from the judge, who nodded.

"As long as justice is done, I'll be satisfied. Into this room, please. I'll want this in writing."

It was a small room with the walls lined with shelves of law books. There was a desk and several chairs. Judge Marland sat at the desk, got out pen and papers.

"Very well, Scudder. Now we'll hear what you have to say."

Once he was committed to it, Rupe Scudder held nothing back. What he gave was a complete refutation of the testimony he'd rendered in court. The words came out of him, heavy, slow, and stumbling. Judge Marland's pen scratched busily. It was, in effect, the same story Antone had given Canby.

When Scudder finished, downcast and sullen, Judge Marland pushed the paper and pen across to him and spoke caustically.

"You'll sign that, Scudder. I suppose Canby has given you some sort of promise of immunity for speaking the truth of this thing, so I'll not interfere with you there. If I had my way, however, you'd know the full penalty for a lying witness. Take him away, Canby. And tell Sheriff Partman I want to see him immediately!"

The town lay quiet under the stars. The wind running down over Pahvant Rim was stronger, carrying the quickening briskness of the high country and now held the far-off fragrance of piñon slopes and the dry incense of distant cedar thickets.

Rupe Scudder was silent until he and Reese Canby reached their horses. Then he mumbled, "I shoulda worked out a trade with you. Don't I get a break?"

"You do," said Canby. "You do because you were just a poor, dumb fool, used as such by Sax Starke and Chelso De Lacca. If you stick around these parts, they're the ones who'll like payment out of your hide. So, if you're smart, you'll travel a long way from here. And next time let the other fellow do his own dirty work."

Rupe Scudder went into his saddle, started to swing away, then checked his horse.

"Starke and De Lacca are dead set on gettin' their hooks into Sentinel Basin," he growled. "They'll stop at nothin' to do it. You're a whiter man than they are, Canby."

Canby waited until the sound of Scudder's horse vanished in the night, then he went around to where Mike Partman's office and jail stood behind the courthouse. The office was dark, so Canby circled back downtown and went into the

Desert House. At this late hour the place was nearly empty.

Tippo Vance, who owned the place and tended his own bar, was sitting at a corner table with Partman and Milt Parrall, playing three-handed cutthroat. When Canby entered, Vance glanced at the empty bar and started to get up. Canby waved him back.

"Stay put, Tippo. Mike, Judge Marland wants to see you. 'Immediately' was the word he used."

Sheriff Mike Partman was a burly man, running to flesh now that the years were beginning to add up on him, and he wasn't seeing the amount of saddle work he'd known in his younger days as a cattle hand. His broad face was pouchy, and his eyes small under heavy lids.

"What the devil could be so important at this time of night?" he grumbled. "Can't a man have a few hours to himself? I got to catch tomorrow's morning stage out, headin' for Yuma with them two Apache bucks."

Canby smiled slightly. "I wouldn't know about that. But I don't imagine the judge's business will take too long. Milt, you keep late hours."

Parrall yawned and stretched. "Advantage of being a bachelor. You're kind of night-hawking it yourself."

"Been busy at this and that," Canby drawled. "What time did the emperor and his following of fools pull out?"

Milt Parrall flushed. "That's not a good line of thought to follow, Reese—that everybody is a fool who don't see things exactly as you do."

"Didn't say that, my friend. But in my book anybody who accepts the teachings of Sax Starke and Chelso De Lacca as gospel certainly needs his head felt. As some may realize before too long."

Mike Partman, heading sulkily for the door, paused and turned.

"A word to the wise, Canby. Lay off tossing fur-rumpling talk to and about Sax Starke and Chelso De Lacca. I heard how you rawhided them today over at the courthouse. As I see it, you're deliberately trying to stir up trouble, and it's my business to head off that sort of thing. I'm telling you to watch your lip."

Canby's smile became sardonic.

"If you don't quit trying to act so noble, you'll have me laughing, Mike. You better shake it up. Judge Marland was pretty impatient."

Behind Canby's smile lay a hovering of frost. Partman saw it, cursed softly, and went on out. Tippo Vance went over to the bar.

"One last one to make you sleep good, boys. On the house."

"Make it small and fast, Tippo," said Canby. "There's something I want to show Milt."

A few minutes later, Canby and Milt Parrall were standing in the outside dark, watching the closed door of Judge Marland's cottage. The door opened, and Mike Partman came out, Judge Marland's final words following him.

". . . and extend the apologies of the Court to those two innocent men, Sheriff . . ."

Mike Partman mumbled some reply, then stamped off toward his office and jail. But only partway. Then he swung around with every evidence of caution and started slipping back downstreet. He halted abruptly as Reese Canby's voice reached him across the star-spangled gloom.

"Jail's the other way, Mike."

Partman's voice was a low, furious note.

"Canby, you're swingin' entirely too wide a loop. Keep your nose out of my affairs."

"Your affairs are my affairs, Mike. I'm one of the people you're working for, remember? John Q. Taxpayer, that's me. Strong for justice and all that sort of thing. I know what Judge Marland told you to do, and he means—now! Let's get at it. Milt and I are sticking around, sort of witnesses to see you do your duty."

Partman's reply was half-strangled.

"I'm telling you to keep out of my business."

Canby walked over to him, and now his tone went cold and abrupt.

"Mike, you and your office will have my respect only as long as you deserve it. But if you turn coyote, as a coyote, I'll brand you, and to hell with whether you like it or not. Now let's go turn Ponco and Dobe loose!"

"I was aiming to turn them loose, damn you!" snarled the badgered sheriff.

"Then you've lost your sense of direction," Canby told him crisply. "Like I said, the jail's yonder, not the way you're heading."

Muttering, Partman swung about, and Canby could smell the dust kicked up by his furious steps. Milt Parrall spoke, mild wonder in his tone.

"I don't get this."

"Simple," said Canby. "Rupe Scudder's conscience got to bothering him. He decided to tell the real truth, and he did, to Judge Marland. I was there, and I heard him. Dobe and Ponco stand completely cleared of that cattle-stealing charge. So the judge has ordered them turned loose now!"

In his office, Mike Partman lit a lamp, got out his keys, and headed down the little hall that connected his office with the jail. In a moment, he was back, followed by two young Apaches, not big men, but straight, lithe figures, their dark faces mask-like but their black eyes bright with wonder. At the sight of Reese Canby, that brightness quickened.

Canby grinned at them and spoke in the Mescalero tongue. They came over to him and gripped his hand. Then, silent-footed, they disappeared into the night.

"Damned cow thieves turned loose so they can steal some more," stated Partman sourly.

"Sing another tune, or you'll have folks laughing at you, Mike," advised Canby. "For there's nothing so stupid as a man who insists on hanging onto a dead cat after it begins to smell. Tonight should teach you one thing, at least. The throne of a self-appointed emperor isn't always as secure as it seems. Come on, Milt."

Out under the stars again, Milt Parrall spoke slowly.

"More behind this than shows on the surface. I'm wondering just when and why Rupe Scudder's conscience got to bothering him? Don't try to flimflam me, cowboy. Rupe Scudder never did have a conscience. But he is the sort, if somebody put the fear of God in him, to open his big mouth and do some talking. Could it have been you by any chance who applied the hot iron?"

Reese Canby laughed softly.

"Let's not go into that, Milt. Main thing is, Scudder talked, and straight for a change. Now I got to leave you. Still more things to do."

"The original busy bee, eh? Listen to a word of wisdom, my friend." Milt Parrall paused, licking a cigarette into shape. "You're storing up a big chunk of trouble for yourself. Contrary to what you may think, Reese, I, for one, am not exactly overly fond of Sax Starke or Chelso De Lacca.

But neither am I underestimating them. I think you are."

Canby shrugged. "I measured them right this trip. I'll keep on trying. I admit I'm a sucker for my friends. I always go overboard there. But neither Ponco nor Dobe nor Antone will ever let me down. Be seeing you, kid."

It was Milt Parrall's turn to listen to Reese Canby ride out of town. Then Parrall headed for the hotel, changed his mind, went down to Pokey Carter's livery barn, got his horse out quietly, and left town himself, heading east.

The cold of very early morning lay over the desert when Reese Canby again rode up to Monument Rock. Newt Dyas's voice reached him, dry and patient.

"What luck, Reese?"

"Good. You can turn Naile loose now. But keep his gun."

Jack Naile's toughness had not diminished. When he got into his saddle, he swung his horse to face them.

"I got a good memory—a damn good memory," he droned. "I'll be remembering you three."

He set the spurs and surged away. Reese Canby went over to where Antone and his men squatted on the chilling sand, patient and stoic. Canby spoke in the tongue he had learned as a boy at Antone's knee.

"The young men are free and have gone back

to their wickiups. When the truth was spoken, the white man's law was fair."

Antone answered in kind.

"An old man thanks you, my son."

He stood up and moved away into the night, his men following like shadows.

"Something you and Newt got on me," complained Sandy Foss sleepily. "You talk Apache as good as they do. Now listen, Reese, please don't tell me you're aiming to head me right out for the Chevrons again. What I crave is to crawl into one of Billy Eustace's hotel beds and sleep for a week."

"You're turning lazy on me, kid." Canby grinned. "But somebody has to head back for the Chevrons, and it can't be me. I got to stick around because this spot is only beginning to boil."

"I'll go," offered Newt Dyas. "Ain't been up in that country for quite a spell. And the old restlessness is bitin' at me. Who'll I tell what?"

"If you mean that, Newt," said Canby, "you can tell Sam McKenzie to take charge and start the herd working back toward home range the first time he sees a dusting of snow on Pizzaro Peak. Stop in at Bob Stent's and take a packhorse load of grub up with you. When Sandy and I pulled out, coffee and flour were getting a little short."

They rode back to town, where Newt Dyas said, "I'll be making an early start. Until I see you again, Reese, keep off the ridge tops! You've got yourself into Sax Starke's hair—tight!"

By midmorning the next day, Reese Canby and Sandy Foss rode out of town. They had had a reasonable sleep and enjoyed the luxury of a shave and a haircut. But Sandy was peevish.

"Here I am all slicked up and smellin' nice of Winey Peebles's best hair oil and you go hustling me right out of town. How am I goin' to keep Mary Stent liking me if I don't see her more than about once in every six months?"

Canby grinned.

"Weren't you the fellow who said living in Cassadora would give a man the jim-jams? I think you were. So what are you kicking about?"

"Visiting for a couple of days ain't living in a place," Sandy grumbled. "What's all the big rush about getting out to headquarters? May be the best part of a month yet before the boys get back home with the cattle."

"Things to do, my lad. Fences to fix, cleaning up of this and that. Winter hay to cut and haul. Always before, I've sent a couple of the other boys in ahead of the herd to get such things done. This time, you and I do it. That makes it a fair shake all around."

Their way ran east out of town, for it was out here that the desert ceased and the black sage foothills began. On their left, the Pahvant Rim curved away in a long, running wall of glowing color, gathering in the fire of the sun until it seemed almost crimson at midday but turning to a maroon brushed with powder blue and purple when the shadows began to build. Its swing was gradually to the north, turning back more and more until distance began to diminish its size and cool its color.

Where a trail broke off the reservation stage road, Reese Canby reined in.

"I'm dropping by to have a talk with Bert Lanifee. Maybe when he gets the full picture of how Starke and De Lacca tried to frame Ponco and Dobe, he'll change his mind about being a string on Starke's fiddle. You amble along and get those chores started. And, Sandy, keep your eyes open!"

The trail Canby took climbed a winding way across the black sage foothills, topped a deceptive crest of country, then swung to a comparative parallel with the long, running drift of the Pahvant Rim. In time, he began passing cattle carrying Bert Lanifee's Trumpet brand. Still farther along, he struck grassy flats between the sage-rumpled hills, and one of these grew until it became a small valley. At the head of this stood the Trumpet headquarters. Several saddle mounts and one buckboard stood beside the cavvy corral fence, and as he swung his own mount in among them, Canby read the various brands thoughtfully.

This same wondering was frowning on his face as he crossed to the ranch house. Here, in a canvas hammock swung angling across one end of the wide porch, Chris Lanifee lay at ease, while in a nearby chair, Mrs. George Winter was busy with a lap full of knitting. Canby took off his hat.

"Ladies! Mrs. Winter, how are you? Chris, how do you keep so cool-looking?"

He scrubbed a shirt sleeve across his brow where his sweat-dampened hair had been pressed tight by his hat.

Chris Lanifee did not answer immediately, but Mrs. Winter fixed somewhat grave eyes on Canby.

"I'm glad to see you show up, Reese. Go on inside and see if you can knock some sense into George Winter's stupid head. I sometimes think that most men are fools before they are anything else. Today, if they let Sax Starke and Chelso De Lacca have their way, I'll be sure of it."

Mrs. Winter's knitting needles clicked faster as she spoke.

A faint flush touched Chris Lanifee's face.

"Bert is pretty level-headed, Mother Winter," she defended.

"My dear," said Mrs. Winter, "in one thing all men are alike. They forget easily. We older women, who went through the Apache wars, will never forget them, and we want no more of them. Go ahead, Reese, do your best."

"Didn't expect to run into a camp meeting," murmured Canby. "Wanted to have a talk with Bert alone." He shrugged. "With your permission, Chris."

Her nod was faintly curt. "Of course. Go on in. If you can keep personalities out of it."

Milt Parrall came out of the house, surprise crossing his face as he saw Canby. He recovered quickly.

"We meet here; we meet there. If you're still carrying the torch, cowboy, leave it outside. There's plenty of sound and fury in there already. Mind if I pull up a chair and look at you, Chris? Be a very pleasant change."

Chris colored slightly but smiled. "Silly!" she murmured.

Reese Canby stepped into the wide and slightly dusky living room of the place. Sax Starke was pacing up and down, talking. Chelso De Lacca was hunkered down against the far wall, the dead stub of a cigarette clinging to his gross underlip. Mason Garr and George Winter had chairs side by side, while Bert Lanifee sat by the center table.

At the sight of Canby, Sax Starke broke off his harangue and his pacing and stood with spread feet. Anger flamed in his eyes.

"Didn't know you'd been invited to sit in on this, Canby."

"Didn't know I had to be," Canby retorted. "For that matter, I didn't know anything like this was going on. I just dropped by for a talk with Bert. Anything wrong with that?"

"Pull up a chair, Reese," said Bert Lanifee.

Canby did so, dropping his hat to the floor beside him and rolling a smoke, while missing none of the somewhat uneasy silence which now settled across the room.

"Don't let me cramp your style, gentlemen," he drawled. "I like to know what's going on. I suppose you've heard that Rupe Scudder admitted to lying witness before Judge Marland and that the judge turned a pair of innocent Apache boys loose?"

As he spoke, Canby looked squarely at Sax Starke and saw the cold anger whip across the man's face.

"That's what we're talkin' about," growled Mason Garr.

"Fine!" approved Canby. "Nice to see everybody willing to admit a mistake."

"We admit nothing of the sort," rapped Sax Starke flatly. "Those two Apaches are guilty as hell. We were also talking of the method you used to coerce Scudder into withdrawing his testimony. That was about as highhanded a piece of business as I've run across in a long time. Who do you think you are, anyway, pulling that sort of thing?"

Canby shrugged. "Sometimes a knife can cut both ways, Starke. Apparently, Jack Naile managed to find his way back to the downy nest. You should give Jack a little talking to, Starke. He's in a fair way to stub his toe."

"Me," put in Mason Garr, "I'm wondering if you told Judge Marland about the kind of pressure you put on Scudder to get him to reverse himself?"

"Didn't have to," answered Canby coolly. "Judge Marland is no fool. He's had lots of experience with liars. And he knew that when Scudder came clean and signed the written statement, he was hearing the truth for the first time since the trial began."

Bert Lanifee stirred restlessly. "You still got that chip on your shoulder, Reese. Take it easy."

Canby inhaled deeply, the angles of his face pulling taut.

"All right, Bert, say I have got a chip on my shoulder. And as long as it's there, this is a good time to get a few things straight and final. I say again that Judge Marland is no fool. And he's an honorable man, calling the cards as he sees them. He wouldn't have freed Ponco and Dobe unless he was fully convinced of their innocence. So if any man in this room tries to claim differently, I say to his face that he's a liar!"

Sax Starke looked at Bert Lanifee, spreading his hands and shrugging. "This is your house, Bert. You're the judge of what can or can't be said here."

Lanifee reddened slightly. "Reese," he snapped, "I'm not warning you again."

"You don't need to, Bert," answered Canby bluntly. "I started to have my say, and I'm going to finish it. Now I don't know how much further you other men are prepared to follow Starke and De Lacca, especially in the light of the cold truth you now know about the dirty deal they tried to put over on Ponco and Dobe. But let's understand one thing clearly and beyond all mistake. Sentinel Basin grass is Apache grass. While I got anything to say about it, it stays that way!"

Sax Starke laughed sarcastically.

"And what do you think you got to say about it? Rating yourself pretty high, seems to me. And I just don't see you as being that big!"

Canby picked up his hat, got to his feet, and looked Starke in the eye. His tone went so cold that his words were brittle.

"I just kicked one spoke out of your wheel, Starke. I can kick more. I know exactly what you're out to do. By any means possible, you and De Lacca are set to stir up trouble enough to push Antone into a false move. You know that if he does, he'll be blamed for everything, rightly or wrongly. You know that you've got the weight of a lot of old hatreds on your side. Justice and fair dealing mean nothing to you. You're smooth enough, apparently, to drag a lot of suckers along with you. In their eyes, you may be quite a guy. But to me, you're a damned, lying, unscrupulous, greedy whelp! There it is, flat in your teeth. Make of it what you want!"

Despite his crippled leg, Bert Lanifee moved with surprising quickness. He was up, snatching at his crutch, using the support of it as a pivot to swing himself between Reese Canby and Saxon Starke.

"Enough of this!" he thundered. "Sax—stay put! I'll handle things."

He turned on Canby, furiously angry.

"I've called you friend, Reese. I've welcomed you into my home. I've asked you decently to keep your name-calling to yourself. You've misused my generosity. You can't seem to get it through your head that I and other men in this room have our complete growth and are quite capable of thinking for ourselves and making our own decisions. You can leave now! And unless you can change your manner, you'd better stay gone. That's my final word!"

Reese Canby met Lanifee's flaming eyes steadily.

"Very well, Bert," he said quietly. "If I've really misused your hospitality, I apologize—to you. As for the rest, I'm not taking back a single damn word! Perhaps in time you'll come to realize that my friendship goes deeper than it seems."

Canby turned and walked out. He saw that Bert Lanifee's furious words had carried clearly to the veranda. Chris Lanifee was sitting stiffly upright in the hammock, her face pale and the shine of anger in her eyes. Milt Parrall was staring studiously at the tip of his cigarette. Mrs. Winter's knitting was idle in her lap, her expression grave and subdued, but with a definite resolve shaping up in her eyes.

Reese Canby crossed the veranda and went down the steps before he turned and looked directly at Chris Lanifee. He was bitterly grave.

"My regrets, Chris. I'm going to try to believe that Bert didn't mean all he said. Mrs. Winter, I did my best. Milt, care to ride with me? Things I'd like to talk to you about."

Milt Parrall stirred slightly, almost uneasily, but he made no move toward leaving.

"Not right now, Reese," he evaded. "Later—maybe."

A hint of weariness shadowed Reese Canby's eyes. He nodded, as though affirming a thought to himself.

"It doesn't matter," he said. "I know now what I wanted to find out. It's always been there, but I wouldn't let myself recognize it. Ladies—!"

He tipped his hat, clanked over to his horse, went smoothly into the saddle, and rode away.

His shoulders were very erect, but there was a shadow of loneliness riding with him.

Mrs. Winter shoved her knitting into a bag by the side of her chair, got to her feet determinedly. She looked directly at Milt Parrall and spoke bluntly.

"I'm ashamed of you, Milt Parrall!" Then she added, to no one in particular, "I allow that man of mine just so much leeway in which to make a fool of himself. After that, I take over!"

She went into the house and presently Chris Lanifee and Milt Parrall heard her say, "There's been one true man in this house today. He just rode away. Now you come along, George Winter. We're going home, too!"

Milt Parrall flipped his cigarette butt across the veranda rail with a trifle more vehemence than was necessary.

"Can't figure what's gotten into Reese," he muttered. "He's making it tough on a lot of us."

Chris Lanifee did not answer. She was watching the disappearing figure of Reese Canby and biting at a red underlip.

Chapter IV
HOVERING STORM

For three weeks, Reese Canby and Sandy Foss did not get two miles away from Canby's Diamond R C headquarters. These were weeks of driving, relentless toil. Canby made them so, working like a man possessed. Everything about the place had to be readied for the return of the herd from its summer range up in the Chevrons. The biggest chore was the cutting, hauling, and stacking of the wild hay which grew in the meadows along either bank of Telescope Creek.

At this, Canby and Sandy worked from daylight to dark, and the sun sweated them down to rawhide and sinew, and they grew sun-blackened and silent under the drive of the job. Sandy said nothing, but more than once he looked at Canby almost resentfully, almost wonderingly, for Canby drove himself without mercy and Sandy felt honor-bound to keep up.

At midmorning one day, they had the last load hauled and stacked. Sandy tossed his hay fork into the wagon and scrubbed a sweat-caked shirt sleeve across his face.

"Been one more acre of that hay to handle, I think I'd have broke down and wept." He looked at his calloused hands. "If I'd had even a mite of sense, I'd have gone back up into the Chevrons, instead of letting Newt Dyas go. Then I wouldn't have been trying to stay even with a crazy man all these weeks. Reese, what the devil's the matter with you? Have you gone money-hungry on me?"

Canby looked at the young puncher, realizing for the first time how Sandy had leaned down, how his face was drawn, and his eyes pulled back into his head. He dropped a hand on Sandy's arm.

"I'm sorry, kid. I didn't think. Or maybe I've been thinking too much. Why didn't you call me before this? You need a couple of days off. Take a ride into town and say hello to Mary Stent for me."

"Oh, I don't figure to run out on you," declared Sandy. "I'm not heading for town unless you come along."

"Yes, you are. The main chore's done. From here on in, there's just odds and ends, with plenty of time ahead. You go on. Clean yourself up and skedaddle. You go in the way you are, and Mary will sic the dog on you."

In the end, Sandy allowed himself to be persuaded, whistling boyishly as he shaved, took a bath in the old galvanized washtub, and got into clean clothes. While he caught up and saddled, Canby leaned against the corral fence, watching him.

“A few things you’re to do and not to do, kid. You’ll look, and you’ll listen, and you’ll bring back a sack of grub. But should you run afoul of Starke and De Lacca or any of that crowd, you’re to keep your mouth shut and not spit in anybody’s eye. Compree?”

“I got my growth,” retorted Sandy. “I can take care of myself. But if that’s the way you want it, that’s the way it’ll be.” He grinned as he went into the saddle.

Canby grinned back. “I don’t want to see hide or hair of you until tomorrow night.”

He watched Sandy until a twist of the lower creek meadows hid him, then he went to the cook shack and put together a frugal meal. The cook shack was full of trapped flat heat, and when he had eaten, Canby went out and squatted in the thin line of shade forming at the northeast corner of the bunkhouse.

It was a favorite spot of his for an after-dinner smoke. From this place, a big sweep of country was visible. From here, he could see the last limit of the long, running curve of the Pahvant Rim, way up there where the lifting sage hills met the darker smudge of the piñon ridges, which seemed to draw in the rim, smother it, and mark its final northern ending. Way out beyond were the Chevrons, running their humpbacked timber blackness across the skyline to some vague infinity.

In that country, Telescope Creek found its beginnings and worked a twisting way down the lower slopes to feed this string of meadows and little basins and make of it a fat parcel of range.

It had cost Reese Canby a lot of work and a lot of time and sacrifice to dig his roots firmly into this chunk of earth. Looking back, he marveled that he had come as far as he had with so little to start with. Well, work could do these things for a man, work and a fair amount of luck. And friends.

How many of these did he have left? This silent question brought a taut bleakness to his face, shadowed his eyes. In town, there'd be a few. Cap Lovelock, Bob Stent, Billy Eustace, Pokey Carter, and, yes, even Tippo Vance in the Desert House. Also, Judge Marland. In the Apache wickiups and jacals about the rim of Sentinel Basin, he'd always be welcome. Antone and his people would never take back their friendship. And Newt Dyas—restless, drifting, solitary Newt—could be depended upon.

But the men of his own calling across the range, the other cattlemen, had drawn a great distance away from him. Saxon Starke and Chelso De Lacca did not matter. At no time had Canby ever known their friendship or wanted it. The rest? Well, here was where the knife cut deep.

The final bitter words of Bert Lanifee still rang in Canby's ears; they had been ringing so since the moment Lanifee uttered them. And Milt Parrall, restless, almost evasive, there on the veranda of the Trumpet ranch house. There had been another twist of the knife. Finally, there was Chris Lanifee, who mattered far more than all the rest put together. Chris would stick by her brother.

It was this realization that Canby had sought to dull and soften by work, driving himself without let-up. Which hadn't done a bit of good. Work might temporarily alleviate punishing thought, but give him a moment of silence, alone, and the thought came back. Like now.

Something registered at the outer edge of Canby's vision. A brief flickering glint in a thicket of willow along Telescope Creek, some two hundred yards above the headquarters. At first, the possible significance of it bounced off the armor of Canby's preoccupation. Sunlight gleaming on the polished horn of a steer, maybe. Only there were no cattle on his range just now. All of his stuff was still up in the Chevrons. For that matter, the gleam had been too bright for horn shine but was more like the glint of the sun on something metallic, like a gun barrel . . .

Reese Canby never knew where the impulse came from that made him throw himself sideways, off his crouching heels, to a full-length flatness on the earth against the sill of the bunkhouse. Yet this was what he did, just ahead of a heavy rifle slug that told solidly against the bunkhouse wall almost exactly where his shoulders had been leaning a split second before. Over in the creek willows, the heavy bellow of a gun report spread rolling echoes.

Canby did not stay flat on the earth. He came up, running, lunging. He beat a second slug to the corner of the bunkhouse by half a stride. With another jump and dive, he was through the bunkhouse door, grabbing at the rifle which hung above Sandy Foss's bunk.

Canby ran the lever back and forth, saw a cartridge feed up from the magazine and slip into the chamber. He whirled and started for the door again but stopped as a third slug whipped in at an angle, splintered the far wall, and went on through, snarling. Whoever it was throwing that rifle lead could not command the door fully, but he could get at it from an angle. And he'd be watching that door.

Canby went down the bunkhouse with long strides, dodging into a corner and flattening himself there. Out in the willows, that rifle took up a measured hammering of report, and whipping slugs searched the bunkhouse from end to end.

Canby heard each slug strike, saw each little burst of splinters whip from the wall, while invisible death buzzed across the long room and went out the far side. Closer and closer moved the splinter bursts, the last one springing from a board not more than a yard from him. Here they stopped, and silence settled in.

He's reloading, thought Canby, and I've got to get out of here. These walls were never intended to stop lead. He's liable to guess the right spot at any second.

There was a window, open, halfway along the south side of the bunkhouse. There was always the chance that another hostile gun, as yet unheard of, might be covering that window. But that was a chance, Canby realized, that he had to take.

Dust, beaten from the walls by the impact of lead, stung Canby's nostrils, made him sneeze. He heard the first slug of this second volley smash into the far end of the bunkhouse. He raced for the open window, swung through it, and dropped close to the earth outside. Over yonder were the corrals, and past the end of them, a ditch twisted in toward the creek.

To reach that ditch, Canby knew he'd have to move into view of that hidden shooter. But once he reached the ditch, things would be different; then he'd be in a position to do something.

He stayed where he was, counting the measured reports of that single gun, hearing the pound and rip of lead through the bunkhouse walls. When the pause and silence for reloading came, he was up and running.

He reached the corrals, swung past the corner

of them, and dived into the ditch. A slug, snapping wickedly close, ripped the edge of the ditch, showering him with dust. Canby crouched, utterly still for a moment, pulling long breaths of relief into his lungs. He was now, at the worst, on even terms in this business.

Up until now, his one thought had been to gain some position like this, where he could begin to hit back; he'd had no time for any other reaction. But with this pause came anger, deep, cold anger, sharpening him to bleakness. He scrubbed the sting of sweat from his eyes and went down the ditch, almost on hands and knees at first, then, as the ditch deepened and widened, at a crouched run.

Where the ditch opened on the creek, a willow clump threw a screen of tangled greenery. Canby dodged into the clear beyond this, paused again. Underfoot, gravel spread white and baked until it reached the moisture-darkened level of the main creek channel at the far side. Upstream lay one willow clump after another, and Canby moved that way, dodging from one clump to another, rifle half raised, ready to smash a shot at the first movement he saw. But he found no target even as he drew close to the spot from which the hostile lead had been winging.

Now, from above and across the creek, came the sudden, surging pound of hoofs, receding swiftly. Distance sucked in the sound, swallowed it completely. The would-be killer had spooked, cleared out. If Canby had had a horse handy, he'd have made a race out of this. But he knew that by the time he got back to the corrals, caught and saddled, the fugitive would be long gone. And to follow too recklessly would be to make an open target of himself to a rifle which might be hidden out and waiting anywhere along the trail.

Still taut and alert, he prowled until he found the exact spot from which the shots had come. Here, nearly two dozen empty rifle shells lay scattered, which told nothing, as they were of a caliber common to the country. In fact, of the same caliber Canby was carrying.

He found the place where the gulcher had tied his horse. Underfoot was soft sand, dry and muffling, leaving no sign that could be read with certainty. And where the horse had clambered up the far bank of the creek were merely a number of long, driving gouges, equally unreadable.

Now, a full, still peace and quiet held the world. Canby settled down by a shaded pool and built a cigarette. The happenings of this past half-hour marked a definite turning point in conditions across this range. Until now, there had been a cropping up of animosities, the rise of ugly possibilities of violence. But always short of actual shooting. Now that point had been passed.

This thing had been no mere attempt at threat. That first sneak shot had had all the deadly intent in the world behind it. Only intuition, unconscious alertness, even something more vague and less understandable than these, had gotten him out of the way of that first try. A split second slower in reaction, and Canby knew he'd be lying over there at that shaded corner of the bunkhouse, drilled through and through. It had become that sort of a world now. With his thoughts, bleakness deepened in him.

There was another angle to be considered. While this past period of violence had been directed at him personally, it could also signify the start of a movement against his entire outfit and against every man of his crew. Like, perhaps, Sandy Foss, only lately headed for town. So somewhere along the trail, or even in town, Sandy might meet up with some of the same. And Sandy was such a kid . . .

Canby went back to headquarters, made a hurried clean-up, caught and saddled, and took the town trail.

The town of Cassadora lay somnolent in its usual midday heat bath. In the coolest corner of Bob Stent's store, Mary Stent busied herself over a lap full of her father's socks in need of darning. Bob Stent himself was away, having gone out by stage the day before on his regular monthly buying trip to Red Mountain.

The shuffle of hoofs sounded, and Mary,

glancing out at the white, heat-beaten dust of the street, saw Chelso De Lacca and two Tepee riders drift past, heading for the Desert House. As they went by, De Lacca swung his gross head, letting his muddy glance play on the doorway of the store.

Mary Stent knew that De Lacca's eyes could not probe far enough past the shadowy doorway to touch her, yet she shuddered. It was an instinctive reaction, as though something unutterably repulsive had glanced her way. Her cheeks burned, and her dark eyes clouded.

Many times in the past had she felt Chelso De Lacca's eyes following her. Never by word or act had De Lacca offered her an affront, but always the impact of his glance left her clammy and sick and shaken. For this man, and everything about him, was foul. Several times, De Lacca had made overtures of friendliness toward her. On one pretext or another, he would come into the store, talk of this or that with Bob Stent, grossly effusive with good nature and heartiness, but always managing, if Mary were present, to get around to talking to her directly. And while outwardly polite, there was always that thing lurking far back in his eyes which left Mary shaken.

Mary had kept her feelings to herself, never even hinting at them to her father or anyone else, for this thing shamed as well as frightened her.

This gross beast of a man, obviously trying to make up to her!

Mary now bit her lip, and her darning needle flew faster. She tried fiercely, as she had tried many times in the past, to tell herself that this was all silly imagination on her part. Deep down, she knew better.

Half an hour of stillness and industry brought back a calmer feeling. But it was only a temporary respite, for there were heavy strides on the porch of the store, and then Chelso De Lacca came in, his glance whipping the warm gloom of the store until it found her. Mary laid down her sewing, left her chair, and retreated behind the bulwark of the counter, trying desperately to keep her manner indifferent and impersonal and to hide the repulsion which swept over her again.

"Mary, howdy!" cxclaimed De Lacca, the moist meatiness of his voice giving an almost slurring effect to the words. "Does beat time how pretty you always look hot day or no. Where others melt down, you never change."

Mary held to the edge of the counter, her knuckles white. She managed to keep her tone even.

"There was something you wanted?"

De Lacca showed his big, stained teeth in what was meant for a confiding grin.

"Well, now, the cook did tell me to order up a sizable list of grub, but that ain't important just now. Mainly, I'm interested in the chance for a nice, quiet talk with the prettiest girl I know. Feller gets fed up with nothin' but the company of rough-headed saddle pounders. You go on back an' sit down. I'll hunker down here, where I can look at you."

Mary could feel the blood burning in her cheeks and was furious with herself because of it. That's it, she told herself silently—so he can look at me.

De Lacca noted the deepening color in Mary's face and was mistakenly encouraged by it. His grin became a confident leer.

"Lots of folks figger me as rough and tough. Well, maybe I am where I have to be. But to a girl like you, I'd be the best of everything. I'd give you all the best that money could buy. I'd set you up in the finest style in the finest ranch house in the country."

He hitched himself up, sitting sideways on the counter, leaned over, and dropped a hand on one of hers. "Why, you and me together, Mary—we'd—"

Mary recoiled, jerking her hand away as though touched by a snake. What was this gross brute of a man talking about? Was he proposing marriage to her? This impossible clod who stank of stale sweat? This—this—!

Fear left her. Blazing anger took its place. Her eyes scorched Chelso De Lacca.

"You'd dare touch my hand?" she cried. "You'd

dare speak to me this way? You filthy—*animal!* Get out of this store. Get out! Don't you ever speak to me or look at me again. Do you hear me? Get out!"

Scalding and outraged as her words were, the revulsion that flamed in her eyes was even more scathing. A more sensitive man than Chelso De Lacca would have shriveled under the impact of it. And, thick-skinned as he was, De Lacca was not impervious.

For a moment, he stared at her, open-mouthed. Then the grime in his muddy eyes thickened, took on a reddish tinge, while his face twisted into a heavy snarl. Mary thought he was coming right over the counter after her.

Swiftly, she moved away, along the back of the counter to where the cash drawer was. On a little shelf beside this, Bob Stent always kept a revolver. Mary caught up the weapon.

"Get out!" she cried again.

Chelso De Lacca slid off the counter and spread his feet heavily.

"So that's how it is, eh?" he growled thickly. "High and mighty. Think you're too good for Chelso De Lacca. We'll see. Before I'm done in this country, you'll crawl to me on your hands and knees. Maybe that Sandy Foss hombre is more to your likin'? Well, I'll take care of that too. Girl, you've stored up something for you and yours!"

He turned and stamped out, but it seemed to the overwrought girl that he left a malevolent shadow behind him.

Mary began to shake. When she tried to put the revolver back on its shelf, she dropped it, the weapon thudding on the floor at her feet. She left it there, went back to her chair, sank into it, covering her face with her hands.

She was furious with herself at what she considered her own weakness. There must have been, she told herself bitterly, better ways of handling things than the one she had taken. But when De Lacca had touched her hand, her revulsion had been too much to control. Something had snapped in her, and she had gone on from there.

Very softly, she began to weep.

A quiet step, the tinkle of a spur, made her look up.

It was Sandy Foss, standing just inside the door. He was lean and brown, clean as a wind from the high hills. Mary came to her feet.

"Sandy!"

He came over to her, the bright, boyish shine of his smile fading and drying up as he saw the tears on her cheeks and the misery in her swimming eyes.

"Mary! What is it? Why are you crying?"

She tried to laugh. It was a weak attempt.

"J-just nerves, I g-guess," she stammered. "Or the heat—and—"

Sandy reached out and took hold of her shoulders.

"No. That's not it. Look at me. You're not the sort to go weepy over nerves. I know you too well. And hot weather never did bother you particularly. Your father—nothing's wrong with him?"

"N-no. Dad's all right. He's at Red Mountain, buying store supplies. Oh, Sandy, I'm so glad to see you! And just forget this silly tantrum of mine. I'm all right now. See—I'm smiling."

Mary *was* glad to see Sandy Foss. In fact, she'd never been so glad to see anyone before in all her life. But she could not hide the almost feverish note in her assurances, or the betrayal of those tears. She was not fooling Sandy in the slightest.

Sandy dropped his hands from her shoulders, began spinning a cigarette into shape. Far back in his eyes, a chill was forming and building up. He spoke musingly, almost to himself.

"I saw him leaving this store just as I rode into town. Chelso De Lacca. He's the cause of this." He looked at Mary almost sternly. "That's right, ain't it?"

Mary realized it was useless to deny. She nodded miserably. Sandy stood, waiting silently. Haltingly, Mary sketched over the affair, making as little of it as possible, leaving out a great deal. But once more, she was not fooling Sandy. He listened, almost impassive, but ever the chill deepened in his eyes.

When she finished, Mary dropped a hand on Sandy's arm.

"You've got to promise me not to make a fuss about it. There was no harm done, really. It's just that the man gives me the creeps somehow. Oh, I'm the silliest of silly fools! Now tell me, what have you been doing since I saw you last?"

"Workin'," answered Sandy laconically. "Reese and me been gettin' things in shape out at headquarters. Which reminds me that I'm supposed to bring back a sack of grub. Might as well get it together now, and then I won't forget it later. No, you stay put, Mary. I know this store well enough to help myself."

Sandy went about stacking grub on the counter. He was doing this deliberately, giving Mary the chance to pull herself together. He moved along behind the counter, lifting down several cans of "airtights," some coffee, and other odds and ends that had grown short on the grub shelf out at headquarters.

His toe struck something on the floor, something hard and heavy and metallic. It was Bob Stent's six-shooter.

Sandy picked up the weapon, held it a moment before putting it back where it belonged. He shot a glance at Mary. She had picked up her sewing again, was fumbling at it, her eyes straight ahead.

Poor kid! She was so much of everything that was completely the best of the world—so bright and merry and full of sparkling good nature when in her normal mood. It must have taken plenty to upset her in this fashion. It wasn't something just of the moment, Sandy felt sure. It was something that had been building up for some time. And here, in a showdown, Mary had had to use the threat of a gun.

Sandy finished laying out the grub order, found an empty gunnysack, stowed the grub in it, took it over, and laid it by the door. He scribbled a list of what he'd taken on a piece of paper, tucked this between the pages of Bob Stent's charge book. Then he sauntered to the door again.

"Be back pretty quick, Mary," he said easily. "Reese told me he didn't want to see me back at headquarters before tomorrow night, so I'm taking my bronc down to Pokey Carter's stable. Last time I was in town, you fed me. My turn this trip. You'll be eatin' supper with me at Billy Eustace's hotel. Be a good girl till I get back."

He was gone before she could object. And he did take his horse down to the livery barn, where he turned it over to Pokey Carter's care. But when he left the stable, it was by the back way, and he circled up along the outskirts of town to come around in above the Desert House. Had he gone back up the street, he knew Mary would see him, guess what he was about, and call him off.

He had done a pretty good job of covering up with Mary, Sandy thought. She'd asked him to promise not to start any fuss because of her unpleasant interlude with Chelso De Lacca, but to that, he'd not given any answer. And he hadn't shown any of the wickedly bright and bitter fury that had gathered in him.

Chelso De Lacca, that heavy-footed, unclean whelp, making himself so objectionable to Mary Stent as to force her to throw a gun on him and to leave her in tears!

Wild, cold, reckless anger such as he'd never known before swelled up in Sandy Foss until it almost choked him.

He came along the alley to the east of the Desert House, turned the corner, and threw one brief glance at the three broncs in front of the saloon all carrying the Tepee brand. Then he pushed through the swinging doors of the place, moved to the end of the bar, hooking a left elbow on top of the mahogany.

Four men were in the place besides Tippo Vance. The four were grouped halfway along the bar, talking and drinking, Chelso De Lacca and his two Tepee riders, Fox Baraby and Al Sheeve. And Sheriff Mike Partman. Chelso De Lacca was doing the least talking but the most drinking.

Tippo Vance came along the bar to Sandy, set out bottle and glass. Sandy poured a full drink, dropped a coin on the bar, and began building a smoke. To Tippo's casually mechanical reference to the weather, Sandy nodded.

"Always hot in this damn town, Tippo."

Sandy was watching De Lacca with a bright, hard challenge. De Lacca pushed out of the little group and moved toward Sandy with his heavy rolling stride. His eyes were so hard and murky they looked like flat buttons of dirty glass stuck in his swart, sweat-slimed face. De Lacca was half drunk but showed it only in the thickness of his voice.

"What she can see in you," blurted De Lacca, "I'll be damned if I know. Well, I told her I'd make you hard to catch, and now's as good a time as any."

Sandy took the brimming glass of whisky and tossed the contents full in De Lacca's face. He tossed words with it.

"You slimy, rotten whelp!"

Chapter V
LYNCH ROPES FOR TWO

Sandy Foss expected Chelso De Lacca to go for his gun and was set for him. Had he been fully sober, De Lacca might have reacted as Sandy figured he would. But the animal that was always in De Lacca became more dominant when he had liquor in him. So now his reaction was purely animal, purely physical. He made no move toward his weapon, but instead drove his heavy bulk headlong into Sandy, hands mauling and clawing.

Despite the liquor in him and despite the bulk of him, De Lacca's move was deceptively fast. The weight of his charge threw Sandy back, drove him crashing into the bar. And De Lacca held him there while he hammered a ponderous blow into Sandy's face.

It was as though the limb of a tree had hit Sandy. For a split second, he was out on his feet, dazed and numbed. Before he could recover, De Lacca had stripped Sandy's gun off of him and tossed it aside.

"With my hands," mouthed De Lacca with obvious relish. "Just with my hands I'll do it!"

He smashed another blow at Sandy.

Only the fact that Sandy was half falling kept the blow from landing squarely. As it was, it skidded along the side of Sandy's head, spinning him half around. But as is the strange way in such things, the second partial blow jarred away some of the numbing effects of the first solid one. The momentary paralysis that had locked Sandy's brain and muscles now left him, and he broke clear of the trap against the bar and had his guard up as he whirled to face De Lacca on more even terms.

Only, at best, these physical terms could never be even. Sandy was outweighed a good thirty pounds, and while De Lacca's physical grossness suggested a ponderousness, it covered an enormous strength and an animal resistance to punishment that was bearlike.

As De Lacca charged in again, Sandy hit him twice and, while the blows pulped flesh and brought blood, they never even slowed De Lacca's rush. Dodging and giving ground rapidly were all that got Sandy clear. He set himself as De Lacca came ponderously around, then threw another punch, threw it as he had never thrown one before. It landed squarely and cut clear to the bone, but it did not drop De Lacca or even stagger him.

It went that way, with De Lacca coming steadily in, with Sandy Foss hitting out with all he had, then having to dodge and duck and spin to get clear. Sandy had the feeling that he was throwing his fists at something that was not human, an elephantine force that kept rolling down upon him and which, despite his mightiest efforts, was due to roll over him and crush him completely.

Tippo Vance looked at Partman and said, "Mike!"

The sheriff shrugged. "Foss started it, didn't he? What did he expect, throwing liquor in Chelso's face? He'll know better next time."

Tippo Vance saw how this thing was going to end, how it must end. He said, "Break it up, Mike, or I will."

"It'll go to a finish far as I'm concerned," growled Partman. "Foss asked for it."

Tippo Vance started around the bar. Fox Baraby slapped an open palm on the bar top, the sound sharp as a gun crack.

"Stay where you are, Tippo!"

Tippo looked into the eyes of Fox Baraby, of Al Sheeve, saw what was there, and shrugged resignedly. But he had his say with Mike Partman.

"You'll never drink in my place again, Mike."

Desperation was in Sandy Foss. It took something out of a man to land a full dozen of the hardest punches he was capable of throwing, any one of them enough to drop an ordinary man, and to find them having no discernible effect other than to reduce Chelso De Lacca's heavy face to a raw and bleeding pulp. The blows seemed to stop there, never getting past the bone structure of the man's head and face, never reaching a nerve or destroying in any way the man's coordination. De Lacca came on and on, steadily, remorselessly.

Whipcord-tough as he was, Sandy felt his strength begin to go. He had put so much into every blow he threw that his energy was burning up fast. Panting breath tore roughly and saltily in his throat. He ducked still another of De Lacca's ponderous swings and ripped both fists to De Lacca's body. It was like hitting a bale of hay. Nothing happened. De Lacca kept coming on.

Nothing, it seemed, could stop Chelso De Lacca, except something that carried more power than lay in a man's fists. A gun—a club—!

Sandy, backing away again, bumped into a poker table. There were chairs also. Sandy half fell over one of these, grabbed at it, straightened, and swung it high. De Lacca drove in before Sandy could bring it down. He jerked Sandy close. He had him at last. Holding Sandy with one hand, De Lacca tore the chair away from him with the other, tore it with such violence that the chair came to pieces and was a useless wreck when it clattered to the floor yards away.

Sandy tried desperately to break loose. His lean, tempered, young body arched and twisted like a steel spring in torment. It was no use.

De Lacca held him, brought down a fist like an oak club. Sandy went numb, his senses beginning to fade. De Lacca handled him easily then. He held Sandy at arm's length with one hand, beat at him again and again with the other.

Sandy went completely out. He hung limply at the end of Chelso De Lacca's arm. And De Lacca beat him and beat him . . .

Over in the store, Mary Stent was listening for the sound of Sandy Foss's light, easy step to signal his promised return. But now it wasn't Sandy's step she heard; instead, it was the heavy, plodding roll of Chelso De Lacca's stride once more. She got to her feet just as De Lacca came through the door.

Mary stared with quick-gathering horror. Chelso De Lacca was a gargoyle. He was smeared with blood, more of it still running down his face, dripping from raw cuts and mashed lips. Over his shoulder, he carried Sandy Foss. Sandy hung limply, like a dead man.

Inside the door, De Lacca paused, feet spread. Words erupted from his smashed, pouting lips with thick, animal grunts.

"See if you like him this way," said Chelso De Lacca.

Then, with what was little more than a shrug of a beefy shoulder, he tossed Sandy Foss to the floor, swung around, and went out.

Mary thought Sandy was dead. She was sure

he was dead. She went over to him with slow, uncertain steps, her hands reaching out toward him, terror and grief shaking her like a leaf in a gale. A strangled whisper broke from her throat.

"Sandy!"

She dropped to her knees, turned him over. He was utterly limp. At the sight of his bloody, beaten face, the barriers gave way.

Mary gathered his head in her arms, careless of the raw blood, and, holding him so, rocked back and forth, her tears a wild flood.

"Sandy!" she sobbed. "Oh—Sandy!"

Up in front of the Desert House, Fox Baraby and Al Sheeve were already in their saddles, waiting for Chelso De Lacca. When he climbed into his saddle, the three of them rode out of town. Mike Partman stood watching them go.

Tippo Vance came out into the street. Partman looked at Tippo, then looked away.

"No sense in gettin' your neck up, Tippo, just because a smart guy found what he was lookin' for. No sense . . ."

Partman's words ran out under the bleak contempt of Tippo's glance. Tippo's reply was as cold as his glance.

"You're a damn yellow rat, Partman. Never come near me again!"

With that, Tippo hurried away, hoping to find Doc Snell in his hotel room.

• • •

Halfway to town, horse moving at a smooth jog, Reese Canby heard a buckboard coming up behind him. He sensed who it would be, and he pulled aside without looking back. Sure enough, Bert Lanifee was driving, and Chris sat beside her brother. They looked across at him as they drew even, and Canby met their glances gravely. He touched his hat.

"Hello, folks."

Bert Lanifee looked troubled but stubborn. Uncertainty lay in Chris's eyes. Both of them noted the fact that a scabbarded rifle was slung under Canby's stirrup leather, an unusual thing. Bert slowed his buckboard team, looking at the weapon.

"That necessary?" he asked gruffly.

"I think so," answered Canby.

"Why?"

Canby shrugged. "A man is never quite sure these days just who his friends are," he said dryly.

Bert Lanifee colored. "You've still got that damned chip on your shoulder."

"Not too long ago, somebody laid out along Telescope Creek in the willows and tried to potshoot me," said Canby. "When things start breaking that way, a wise man takes precautions."

Chris Lanifee paled slightly. "You mean, Reese, somebody took a shot—at you?"

"Nearer twenty of them. Had me dodging and ducking pretty lively for a time."

"That," said Canby, with slow, cold meaning, "is something I sure would like to find out."

Neither of them could miss the gray frost that hardened Canby's eyes or the taut temper that sharpened the lean angles of his face.

Bert Lanifee growled irritably. "I don't know what's come over this damn country."

Canby smiled mirthlessly. "Oh yes, you do, Bert. You know what it is just as well as I do. You seem partial to it, too."

Bert Lanifee swore, slashed his whip, and the buckboard team surged away. Canby watched until the rolling dust cloud hid the vehicle and its occupants, then he took up his jogging way.

When Canby reached Cassadora, he saw the Lanifee buckboard tied in front of the hotel. He reined over to the rack in front of Bob Stent's store. Just as he dismounted, he saw Doc Snell coming out of the store, business satchel in hand.

Doc Snell was a slight, agile little man beginning to grizzle.

"Somebody under the weather, Doc?" asked Canby. "Bob Stent, maybe?"

"Not Bob Stent," answered Doc crisply. "Sandy Foss."

Canby stiffened, tying up a little inside. "What's the matter with Sandy?"

"In my time," said Doc, "I've seen some

beat-up men. But never anything like this. Nobody ever came nearer being killed by raw, brute power than Foss was. He missed what could have been a fatal concussion by a thin whisper. I got him under an opiate now, and when that wears off, he should be out of the woods. I sometimes wonder why the Lord put four legs on some animals and only two on others. That Chelso De Lacca . . . !" Doc went on, shaking his head.

The store was empty. Canby knocked softly on the rear door that led to the Stent living quarters. Mary Stent answered his knock. This girl, usually so vivid and sparkling, was ghost pale, eyes red from weeping.

"Where is he?" asked Canby grimly.

Without a word, Mary led the way to her father's room. Sandy lay quiet between clean sheets, deep in the inert sleep of the opiate. His face was blackened with bruises and swollen all out of shape. A plaster bridged his nose, pulling it back into shape, for one of Chelso De Lacca's ponderous blows had broken it. Another plaster drew together and covered a wicked cut along the left eyebrow. Sandy's lips were puffed and split.

For a long time, Reese Canby stood quiet, looking down at this lean young puncher of his. The frost in his eyes became ice. He turned away. There was nothing he could do here. Doc Snell had done all that could be done. In the kitchen, Canby faced Mary Stent.

"How did it happen, Mary?" he asked gravely.

Mary sat by the table, dabbing at her eyes. In low, muffled tones, she told as much as she knew. "It's all my fault," she ended. "When Sandy said he was going to put up his horse, I might have known what he really meant to do. I should have stopped him."

"Knowing the kid, I doubt you could have, Mary," said Canby. "In his place, I'd have done the same." He dropped a hand on her shoulder. "Buck up. In a few days, Sandy will be as good as ever. And it's not your fault. Some of us have been a little blind about things, I guess, but no longer. Yeah, get your chin up. Everything will be all right."

He put a finger under that soft, quivering chin, tipped her head back, and smiled down at her. "If Sandy saw you this way, then he would feel bad. So get that old sparkle back. I'll be around to help you keep an eye on the kid tonight. Now I think I hear somebody out in the store."

The customer was Chris Lanifee. She looked at Canby and Mary a little sharply as they came in the back way, Canby's comforting hand still on Mary's shoulder. Mary was dabbing a last stray tear from her eye.

Meeting Chris's glance, Canby said, "You and Bert going to be long in town, Chris?"

"Depends," answered Chris, her manner a trifle stiff. "Why?"

"Mary's got Sandy Foss tucked away in back. Be kind of nice of you to give her a hand in nursing him."

"What's the matter with Sandy Foss?"

"He ran afoul of a two-legged animal and got the licking of his life. Maybe licking is the wrong word. Too mild. Mauling is better. Yeah, a mauling by a two-legged animal. Chelso De Lacca."

Some of the stiffness left Chris's manner. "What—what did they fight about?"

"I'll let Mary tell you that," said Canby.

Canby went out and headed for the Desert House. The gentler manner he had shown in the store now completely evaporated. He was hard-jawed when he turned into the Desert House. Bert Lanifee was there, along with Milt Parrall, having a beer. Tippo Vance had been telling them something.

Canby spoke harshly. "You can start all over again, Tippo, and tell it to me. I want the whole picture—about Sandy Foss and Chelso De Lacca. All of it!"

Tippo told it.

"A fight's a fight," rapped Canby, "up to a certain point. When it gets close to murder, there's a time to stop it. You say Mike Partman was here. Why didn't he do something about it?"

Tippo shrugged. "I told him to stop it. I could see what it was coming to right at the start. I told Partman twice to stop it, but he wouldn't do a thing. Then I set out to do something about it myself. But there was Fox Baraby and Al Sheeve ready to throw a gun on me. So all I could do was stand there and watch it. It wasn't pretty. I told Partman what I thought of him. Then I went after Doc Snell."

Tippo Vance's eyewitness story of the thing had been terse but graphic, brutally direct. Canby could fairly see Sandy Foss, already completely senseless, being held erect by De Lacca while he beat the kid and beat him.

Canby turned abruptly to Bert Lanifee and Milt Parrall.

"Well, how do you two like that picture? Nice hombre—De Lacca. Good friend of yours, ain't he?"

Milt Parrall said nothing, and in the glance Canby threw at him was a tinge of reluctant contempt. Once, not so long ago, he had sincerely liked Milt Parrall and valued him as a friend. But there was an evasiveness in Parrall that was becoming more and more evident.

Bert Lanifee still kept his stubborn look.

"I agree with you that Chelso might have gone a little further than was necessary," he growled. "At the same time, let's not forget that Foss threw a glass of liquor in Chelso's face. Was a man to do that to me, I might go pretty rough myself."

"It's too damn bad the kid didn't throw a couple

of forty-five slugs instead of the liquor," retorted Canby harshly. "But that's a chore I may take care of. Tippo—thanks!"

Canby turned and went out, heading now around the courthouse to Mike Partman's office and jail. Canby heard a desk drawer close as he reached the sheriff's office door, but when he stepped into the place, the smell of whisky was in the air. Mike Partman, flushed and truculent, leaned back in his chair.

"I know what you're goin' to say, Canby," he half-snarled. "But keep it to yourself. I'm sick of being told my business. When smart guys hunt trouble and find it, that's their hard luck. It's not my chore to wet-nurse every wise cowpoke who gets his roach up and sets out to make a damn fool of himself."

Canby set about rolling a smoke, his narrowed glance boring at Partman. He let Partman have his say and made no answer until the cigarette was between his lips and glowing, then he spoke evenly.

"When a rough game begins to shake into place, I like to know where everybody stands. Sometimes it's a little hard to pin the slippery ones down. But I got you figured, Mike. You're not a sheriff. You're not even a thin imitation of one. You're a damned, crooked, gutless poodle dog, ready to lie down and roll over any time Sax Starke or Chelso De Lacca wants to snap a finger at you. I suggest you resign and turn in your star, because I'm going to run you out of this country, Mike. You've already played Starke and De Lacca's game too long to ever come out with a clean neck. You stay in it any longer, and you'll end up behind bars—if you're lucky. If your luck runs out, well—!" Canby let a shrug finish for him.

Cold sober, Partman might have been warned by the gray chill of Reese Canby's manner. But Partman had sopped up just enough liquor to give him some small measure of false backbone. He bounced to his feet, blurting furiously.

"You got your damned nerve, coming into my own office and throwin' that kind of talk at me, Canby. You can't threaten me. I'll show you that you can't!"

"Sit down, Mike!"

"I'll show you—"

"Sit down!"

The words were like a whiplash. Reese Canby took a step forward.

Liquor nerve had no show against the real thing. Mike Partman dropped back into his chair. Canby moved up to the desk, spread his hands on it, leaned forward, and stared bleakly down at Partman.

"Today," he gritted, "out at my headquarters, a dry-gulcher made a try for me. I'm telling you this, not because I expect you to do anything about it, but just so you'll get the picture clear.

Yeah, somebody tried to get me from the willows along Telescope Creek. I don't take that sort of thing sitting on my heels, Partman. If I thought you had enough guts and honesty in you to do something about that kind of business, I'd be only too glad to turn the whole deal over to you. Just so you can't say I'm not fair about this, I'm going to give you this chance to show what you are or what you're not."

Canby paused, pulled a deep inhale from his cigarette, and tossed it aside.

"You know as well as I do what camp that dry-gulcher came out of. I'm suggesting you ride out there and read the riot act to them. A real sheriff would do that very thing. We'll see now whether you're a real sheriff. Well?"

"If you don't know for sure who took a shot at you, how do you expect me to?" mumbled Partman. "As for sayin' any one outfit was responsible, that's damn foolishness. You got to have some shadow of proof before you go chargin' anybody with somethin' like that. Could have been most any stray. How do I know how many enemies you got or how many friends? Hell, you're askin' me to go chase a shadow."

Canby's smile was hard and mirthless. "I'm finding out about my enemies—and friends. Quite an education. But a word of caution here and there wouldn't hurt any, Mike. Don't you agree?"

"I'll do what I can," agreed Partman sulkily. "But I'm saying right now that if you'd had sense enough to mind your own business, you wouldn't—" Partman broke off, began to flounder.

"Ah!" murmured Canby sardonically. "You can put two and two together, can't you, Mike? Well, I'm leaving it up to you—this time."

He turned and prowled out. Mike Partman stared at the empty doorway for some time, and the light in his pouchy eyes took on the hard glitter of hate. He opened a desk drawer, took another gulp at the whisky bottle he unearthed, and drove the cork back in with a hard slap of his palm.

"That's just it," he muttered thickly. "You wouldn't mind your own business, and you won't. So you'll take what you get, Canby. But just to make things look good—"

He got up, lifted down a belt and gun from a wall peg, and buckled it on. Then he went down to Pokey Carter's livery barn, saddled his horse, and rode out of town.

Reese Canby, sitting on the porch of Billy Eustace's hotel, watched him go.

Billy Eustace, holding down his usual spot, slowed the creaking of his rocking chair and inquired softly, "Now, why all the industry of our estimable sheriff, Reese? Must be something real important to start him riding in the middle of a hot afternoon."

A faint smile thinned Canby's lips across his teeth. "When the small, crooked mind gets befuddled and uncertain, Billy, it seeks comfort from the master intellect."

The hotel-keeper laughed soundlessly. "You're good for me, Reese. Wish you'd come around more often."

Bert Lanifee appeared on the porch of the store, came heading for the hotel, swinging his crutch.

"Always hurts me to see a man as strong and vigorous as Bert Lanifee was tied down to a crutch for the rest of his days," murmured Eustace. "That's what a fractious horse can do to a man. You can't entirely blame Bert if he flies off the handle now and then. You and me might be even harder to get along with were we in his boots, Reese."

Canby nodded gravely. "I keep remembering that, Billy."

As he stumped up the hotel steps, Bert Lanifee said, "Chris and I will be staying over, Billy. The usual rooms, if they're empty."

"They're empty, Bert." Eustace nodded. "Happy to have you, as always."

Bert Lanifee looked at Canby. "Chris is going to give Mary Stent a hand with Sandy Foss," he explained gruffly. "I see Mike Partman heading out. Something in the wind?"

"Going to investigate that dry-gulcher deal—he says."

Bert Lanifee stared at the street. “The other day, out at my place, I didn’t mean all I said, Reese. The trail to Trumpet is open to you, same as always. I think you knew that right along.”

“I think I did.” Canby nodded. “But it’s good to hear you say it. Pull up a chair and help Billy and me hold this porch down.”

Bert shook his head. “Promised Milt Parrall I’d be back for a rubber game of pedro.”

Lanifee went over to the Desert House.

Chased by a haze of dust, the Red Mountain stage came rolling in. Bob Stent got down and went into his store. Reese Canby got his horse and took it down to the livery barn. He intended to hold down some of the night watch over Sandy Foss himself.

The afternoon ran out its hot length, sundown flamed, and then the blue of twilight soothed and gentled the world. Reese Canby had supper at the hotel and headed for Bob Stent’s store to arrange with Mary Stent and Chris Lanifee about taking over his share of the night watch at Sandy Foss’s bedside. He was crossing the store porch when Chris came out.

“How’s Sandy doing, Chris?” asked Canby.

“Very well, I think. Dr. Snell was in to see him again just before supper. He’s still sleeping.” She hesitated a trifle, then added, “Walk a little with me, Reese.”

They struck off downstreet, past the livery

barn. Cap Lovelock, sitting with his pipe in the doorway of his saddle shop, waved to them through the thickening dusk.

Canby kept his silence, acutely conscious, as always, of this slender, smooth-striding girl beside him, waiting for her to talk. When she did, it was with an almost childlike eagerness and candor in her words and manner.

"Sometimes all of us can be stupid, Reese. Bert and I were the other day at home. We treated you, an old friend, pretty shabby. I wanted you to know I've been sorry about that, and I know Bert has too. Old friends should never act that way toward each other." She let out a little sigh. "There! Now I feel better."

Canby laughed softly. "So do I—plenty! Somebody who went away for a little while has come back to me. This is the old Chris Lanifee."

"Then how about the old Reese Canby putting in an appearance again, so I won't be afraid anymore."

"Afraid! You?" scoffed Canby. "Even if you were, what have I got to do with it?"

"A great deal," she declared. "Reese, I don't want to see trouble come to this range. And if you don't start any, why, then there won't be any."

Some of Canby's newly-found contentment dried up.

"I don't quite get that, Chris. There was that dry-gulcher affair today. I didn't start that. Why,

I haven't been off my own range for the past couple of weeks. Yet somebody tried to dry-gulch me. What's your answer to that?"

She hesitated a moment. "Couldn't that be a holdover from an earlier argument?"

Canby's tone went a trifle bitter. "If it is, then it's a pretty strong indictment against certain people. Gulching is a mighty dirty business. Chris, you're slipping away from me again. In your eyes, I'm still a culprit. Who are you trying to excuse, and why?"

She stood silent, biting her lip. She spoke slowly.

"Did it ever strike you that it might be your own safety I'm concerned about? It's one thing to take on a fight when the odds are reasonably even. It's something else to charge recklessly into an affair you can't possibly win. Even if the weight of justice is all on your side, that isn't good judgment, Reese."

"Where certain principles are involved, odds don't count, Chris."

"I looked at Sandy Foss lying there, terribly beaten," she said with troubled softness. "He got that way—for what?"

"Mary Stent told you why Sandy tackled De Lacca, didn't she?"

Chris flushed. "Yes. But—"

"Mary had to grab a gun to keep De Lacca in his place," cut in Canby. "Knowing that, I'd have disowned the kid if he hadn't had a try at De Lacca. A whipping—what's that? Every man has to take a whipping now and then. No disgrace in that. The disgrace would be in dodging one when plain, decent principle demands that you go in swinging. As for De Lacca, I expect to have a little talk with that slimy brute."

"That's just it!" cried Chris. "That's the sort of thing I'm afraid of." She caught Canby's arm. "Oh, please understand me. I think De Lacca is a foul animal, too. I always have. But he's dangerous, Reese. And if you go after him—"

At the east end of the street, a murmur of speeding hoofs suddenly became a hard, driving pound, suggesting some dire urgency. Canby dropped a hand on Chris's slim one, turned an alert head, listening.

The hoofs came to a clattering halt. There came an indistinguishable lift of voices. The rack of hoofs began again, came as far as the livery barn, then Newt Dyas's voice calling across to Cap Lovelock.

"Seen Reese Canby, Cap? Billy Eustace said he came this way."

Before Cap could answer, Canby lifted a call.

"Out here, Newt!"

Chris Lanifee pressed a little closer to Canby. "He brings trouble," she cried softly. "Why must they always come to you?"

Newt came afoot, running. At the sight of

Chris, he pulled awkwardly at his hat. "Sorry, Reese. Didn't know you weren't alone."

"That's all right, Newt," Canby told him. "What's up?"

Newt hesitated, still looking at Chris. Then he shrugged. "Bad business, Reese—plenty bad! Coming back from the Chevrons, I cut around and came down through Sentinel Basin. I shot an eagle back in the Chevrons, and I brought the feathers down for the Apache kids. They like to dress up in 'em. Well, Antone's camp was in an uproar. With reason. Reese, somebody lynched Ponco and Dobe!"

"What! Ponco and Dobe—lynched?"

"That's right," said Newt wearily. "A cougar had begun to work along the north rim of the basin—killed two or three calves. Dobe and Ponco went out to try to get the brute. They'd gone three days. Antone got to wondering, so he sent a search party out. They found Ponco and Dobe hanging from the same tree. Reese, Antone is getting ready to ride. And that'll be hell!"

Chapter VI
SOMBER PROMISE

For a long moment, Reese Canby stood very still. It seemed as though a gray chill had swept down off Pahvant Rim and engulfed all of this night that had been warm and still and soft breathing. Words broke from Canby, bitterly harsh.

"The fools! The arrogant, stupid fools! This means more dead men than two. This means—!"

He turned back uptown, drawing Chris Lanifee with him, walking so fast Chris almost had to run to keep up with him. Over his shoulder, he said to Newt Dyas, "In the stable, Newt. My bronc. Saddle it. Get a fresh horse for yourself. Bring them over to Judge Marland's place. Hurry it! We got no time to lose."

Just short of Bob Stent's store, Chris Lanifee managed to pull Canby to a halt. She tried to keep her voice steady but didn't do too good a job of it.

"It—it's terrible, Reese—that lynching, I mean. I know what it can start. But you—do you have to—?"

"Yes, Chris, I do," cut in Canby. "This is no time for conceit, so I'm not showing any. But, Chris—there's just two men who can stop Antone from turning red wrath loose across this range.

Those men are Newt Dyas and myself. One thing you must promise me. Keep Bert out of this! Understand—keep him out of it. Don't let Starke or De Lacca or Mason Garr or anybody else talk him into taking sides. Make him stay neutral. You can do it. You got to do it. You got to help me in this, Chris—!"

He caught her by both shoulders and stared down at her. He saw her head nod tautly as her answer came up to him.

"I promise, Reese. I promise—"

Canby left her so, heading for Judge Marland's cottage almost at a run. Chris stood just as she was for a long moment, her hands clasped and twisting in front of her, then she went into the store.

In the black shadow at a corner of the store, there was soft movement, then Milt Parrall stepped out into the starlight. He swung his head toward the store door, then back upstreet where Reese Canby was hurrying. Parrall's cigarette winked hotly bright as he took a deep inhale, then was a fluttering, arcing glow as he flipped it aside. Parrall slid across the street and disappeared in the dark.

Reese Canby faced Judge Marland across the desk in the latter's little study. And while Canby talked, Judge Marland's eyes frosted with anger and concern, and his face turned grim.

"So there it is, Judge," ended Canby. "There is

just one way in which we can stop Antone from turning his braves loose to spread red hell. That way is to convince him that the white man's law will run down that lynch crowd and exact punishment. And then make good on the promise. I know and you know that Mike Partman won't do this. He's a sheriff in name only. Beyond that, he's just a stupid tool of Sax Starke and Chelso De Lacca. We've got to act fast, Judge. We've got to cut corners and really move."

Judge Marland nodded gravely. "Yes, Canby, you're right. What do you suggest?"

"I'm going out to see Antone now. I'm going to make him that solemn promise that those who lynched Dobe and Ponco will be brought to justice, then I'm going to set out to do it, I am. I'll make my authority as I go along. I'll use whatever means I have to to make good. I'm sure to get way outside the letter of the law. There'll be those who'll come to you asking for my scalp. I'm not going to try to influence your official judgment. I'm just talking to you as a man old enough and sane enough to understand fully what this thing can lead to if it gets out of control. I got friends on both sides, Judge. And I'm just as anxious to keep Antone's people from getting hurt as I am a bunch of innocent white folks. I hope I go away with your permission to act as I see fit, Judge."

The judge spoke slowly. "My life has been

dedicated to the purpose and proper interpretation of the written law. But I remember the days of the Apache wars. I want no more of such. Good luck, my boy! I won't let you down. You can depend on that."

Judge Marland put out his hand, and Canby grasped it, then he whirled and was gone.

Outside, Newt Dyas came hurrying up with the horses.

"One more chore, Newt," explained Canby, "then I'll be with you."

Canby hurried over to the Desert House. Only one person was there besides Tippo Vance. Milt Parr leaned against the bar, toying with a whisky glass. Canby caught him by the arm.

"Don't know as I ever asked you a favor before, Milt. I'm asking one now. Locate somebody to ride up into the Chevrons and tell my crew to start the herd for home right away—and don't spare the horses. Will you do that?"

Milt Parrall's eyes were slightly veiled. He drained his glass before answering, then nodded as he put the glass down.

"Good boy!" said Canby.

Parrall stared at the doors until they quit winnowing from Canby's leaving, then he shoved his empty glass across the bar for another filling. This done, he carried the glass over to a poker table, sat down, and began laying out a hand of solitaire.

For some little time, Tippo Vance moved up and down behind the bar, polishing the mahogany, cleaning a glass or two. From time to time, he glanced at Milt Parrall. Finally, he spoke.

"Reese sounded like it was pretty urgent about getting that word to his crew, Milt."

Parrall shrugged without looking up. "Canby likes to make everything sound like it's important. No rush."

Tippo Vance squared around, his hands spread on the bar. Cool contempt shone in his eyes.

"Milt," he said steadily, "I think you better go somewhere else to drink your liquor and play your cards."

Parrall swung his head, held Tippo's glance for a moment. "Now you're talking and acting foolish, Tippo."

"Maybe," agreed Tippo briefly. "But I mean it. Get gone and stay gone, Milt. You don't need to send the word Reese asked you to. I'll attend to that myself."

Parrall came up suddenly, snarling. "You damn fool! You're asking to get yourself run out of this town."

Tippo shrugged. "Maybe. But not by you. I'll take my chances with the men in this country, not with the coyotes. Git! You don't owe me anything for those last two drinks. They were worth it to find out the true color of your hide—and to get rid of you. On your way!"

Tippo's eyes were too cold for Parrall to face. He left, cursing with every step.

Reese Canby and Newt Dyas slashed out the miles on sweating horses. The animals were lagging with weariness by the time the lights of Reservation came into view. Canby and Newt did not pause in this bleak little town, which was the leftover of the days when it was the headquarters of Reese's father as Indian agent. Here, as a boy, Reese Canby had played with Ponco and Dobe and other Apache kids. With Ponco and Dobe . . .

Ahead, the black sage hills lifted to a crest beyond which lay Sentinel Basin. Short of the crest, Canby and Newt swung away along a side road that broke suddenly over into a little valley where cottonwoods fringed a frugal stream.

They slowed at this crest and went on at a walk. Abruptly, a mounted figure was before them. Canby spoke swiftly in the Mescalero tongue. The figure drifted from sight, and the road lay open again. Dropping down the valley slope, Canby could see no flicker of light anywhere. But presently, in the pale starlight, he picked up the squat bulk of wickiups and the more gaunt outlines of a jacal here and there.

Silence that was not silence lay over the Apache village. It was something a man did not hear with his ears. Instead, it was something that a man felt, a suspended something that bristled the hair on the back of a man's neck.

Dark figures seemed to rise from the ground, stopping Canby and Newt Dyas fully. Canby spoke again in the Apache tongue, slowly, carefully. Finally the Apache guard let Canby through but held Newt Dyas where he was.

One of the guards went with Canby, leading him to a jacal which stood somewhat apart from the others. Starlight lay white around it and here and there faintly pierced through the roof of cottonwood boughs. Canby barely made out the dark figure sitting there, the figure that was Antone.

"I came as soon as I heard, Antone," said Canby gravely.

Antone's answer was dry, whisper thin. "You are welcome, my son. Come and sit with an old man in his grief. Your brothers lie beside you."

Now, in that elusive half gloom, Canby made out two still, blanket-covered figures. Ponco and Dobe. Whom he'd played with as a kid. And friends always, through the lifting years.

"There are tears in my heart," said Canby simply as he dropped on his heels beside the old chief.

"What word do you bring, my son?" asked Antone presently.

"I have come to plead with your wisdom and to bring you a promise," Canby told him. "The old ways must not come back, for that would mean ruin everywhere. My promise is—justice. I will track down those who did this thing and strike justice with my own hand. In your wisdom, you will understand why it must be this way."

"I am old and tired," said Antone. "I want only peace. But the fires are burning in the young men."

"Your word is tribal law, Antone. You must quench those fires. You must believe me, the young men must believe me. Justice will be done. I swear that!"

For a long time, Antone was silent. Canby, listening, could hear the breathing of the village all about him. He felt it like a man felt starlight, even though his eyes be closed. In it was the anger of the young men, the weariness of the old. In it was the rocking grief of the women, the fretful whimpering of the children. In it were wild hearts crying at injustice, crying as they had so many times before. In it was the voice of a people, wanting only fairness.

Finally, Antone spoke. "I believe, my son."

The tautness ran out of Reese Canby. He wiped the sweat from his face. He had not realized until now how tightly locked everything had been within him. So much had been riding on this. The admiration he'd always had for this old Indian sitting beside him deepened.

"Your wisdom is as wide as the night," he said simply.

Dawn was not far off when Reese Canby and

Newt Dyas rode away from the Apache village. Canby had talked long with Antone, getting all the story, getting also directions. These led Canby and Newt Dyas into Sentinel Basin, and in the gray-and-rose dawn, they crossed this great sweep of grass country where the Apache herd grazed and fattened. They reached and climbed the rugged northern slope of the basin into country where the piñons and the pines came down. Here, Newt Dyas, as good as any Apache at reading sign, found the tree.

For some time, Newt studied the ground round about, then he reconstructed the picture.

"That limb," he said, pointing. "They hung them both to that limb. They brought them up under it, still on their horses. They noosed them, then ran their horses out from under them. See here?"

Newt pointed to hoofmarks, gouged deep, where startled ponies, smarting under a sudden quirt lash, had surged forward, out from under the two Apache herders who had ridden them.

Canby nodded, cold-eyed. "We'll backtrack, Newt."

"We'll have to," said Newt, "to do any good. After the lynching, they scattered."

Newt took the lead, eyes on the earth. The trail led to a frugal camp, where Dobe and Ponco had been surprised and captured. Here, Newt got down and worked around again.

"Five," he announced presently. "Five in the lynch party."

"The five I want," said Canby harshly. "Let's go!"

They kept on working out the backtrack. There was something about it that puzzled Newt for a time. Presently, he found the answer.

"One man discovered Ponco and Dobe's camp," he said. "He went back, got the others, then brought them in."

"That adds up." Canby nodded. "Five men would hardly have been ramming around up here together just for the ride. But one man could have been on the prowl, scouting, waiting for some opportunity like this. Waiting for any opportunity," he added, remembered the bushwhacking attempt that had been made against him.

Thc trail led higher into the rough country, then sharply west until it reached a point from which Canby and Newt could see the Pahvant Rim, blazing with color under the climbing sun. From here, they could also mark the twisting line of greenery, which was Telescope Creek, and spot the dwarf bulk of ranch buildings, which was Canby's headquarters. Farther south, tucked close under the curving shoulder of Pahvant Rim, they picked up the glint of sunlight on window glass, which was Bert Lanifee's Trumpet headquarters.

The trail broke that way, angling and swooping across the slopes of the lower hills, finally crossing one of Bert Lanifee's meadow pastures and cutting into the dusty town trail from Trumpet.

"They played it smart, Reese," said Newt. "The sign is beginning to blur and mix up already in this trail. If they stick to it until it breaks into the Reservation Road, and I'm betting they will, we've drawn an empty sack."

This proved true. No sign remained long on the Reservation Road. What with a daily stage over it, along with a certain amount of rider traffic, this dusty way sopped up and hid hoofprints in a matter of hours.

Canby stared up and down the road with hard eyes. Newt said, "We could work up and down the road on either side, looking for a turnoff. But that wouldn't prove much, if anything, even if we found one. There's bound to be a gap which we'd have to fill in with guessing, and guessing wouldn't get us anywhere."

Canby nodded. "I should have known it wouldn't be simple. I see smooth scheming behind this, Newt. We'll have to meet it with some of the same. We might as well get back to town."

They rode for half a mile in silence. Then Canby said gravely, "You know what this can lead to, Newt. Maybe a slug in the back, any time, any place. I gave Antone my own promise, but you don't have to buy in, you know."

Newt stared straight ahead, through squinted eyes. "If it's good enough for you, it's good enough for me," he observed in his dry, quiet way.

Back in Cassadora, Newt took over the horses while Canby went straight to. Bob Stent's store. The storekeeper showed open relief when Canby stalked in.

"How's Sandy?" Canby asked.

"Doing fine. You're the one I want to see, Reese. The town's full of all kind of talk—about that lynching. I've been wondering what the facts are and if there's anything to the rumor that Antone is making ready to pick up the rifle again?"

"Antone isn't picking up any rifle," answered Canby. "You can scotch that rumor right now, Bob. In fact, go out of your way to scotch it, because that kind of talk is dangerous talk. There's nothing to it. I had a talk with Antone last night, so I know what the story is."

"I'm glad to hear that," said Stent. "From what Milt Parrall said, I thought—"

"Milt doesn't know anything about it," cut in Canby. "Anything he says is secondhand stuff he's got from somebody else."

The storekeeper was eying Canby closely. "You got a look about you, Reese. The rawhide is showing."

"I didn't get any sleep last night." Canby

shrugged. "Maybe that's it. Well, I'm going in and say hello to Sandy."

Sandy was awake, resting easy, with Mary Stent puttering about the room. Canby gave her a grave smile.

"Hi, nurse! Can I talk to the patient, or is he too busy holding your hand?"

Mary flushed. "He's an ungrateful scamp," she charged. "Here, after scaring the wits out of us all, he's ready to swear at me because I won't bring his clothes and let him get up and about again. And he knows that Dr. Snell said he's not to leave that bed for at least two days."

"I'll take care of that," promised Canby.

He stood beside the bed, looking down at his young saddle hand. Sandy's least discolored eye peered up from among his bandages, reasonably bright and cheerful.

"Hell of a way for a man to spend his life, hey, boss?" he mumbled. "Flat on his back in bed, all tied around with bandages. See if you can argue with Mary for me. Never knew she could be so stubborn."

"I'm not arguing with anybody but you," growled Canby. "For that matter, I'm not arguing with you. I'm just telling you. Mary's the boss here. Whatever she says goes. Understand?"

Canby's growl faded to a smile. "Learn anything, kid?"

"Plenty!" admitted Sandy. "Bare hands is

good enough against some specimens. The other kind—well, a sawed-off shotgun is the medicine there."

"Keno! Never forget that. But I'm kind of proud of you, kid. Now quit naggin' at Mary, do as you're told, and in a week I'll have you pitching hay again."

"Huh!" grunted Sandy. "Not me. I've parted company with a hayfork for good and all. Running the misery end of one of them things is what weakened me down so I couldn't hit harder. Reese, it was like punching a wall. Never try it hand-to-hand with De Lacca. Use a club, and a stout one."

A cold flash hardened Canby's eyes. "I got an angle or two figured out, kid." He turned to the girl. "Might there be still a cup of coffee left in the pot, Mary?"

"If there isn't, there will be. Come along."

In the kitchen Canby let himself down into a chair with an unconscious sigh, slouching deep, his big shoulders loose and sagging in relaxation.

Mary, busy at the stove, said, "The talk going around scares me, Reese. That lynching—what a cruel, dreadful thing! And now the Apaches will—"

"The Apaches are sitting quiet, Mary," cut in Canby. "They'll stay that way. I have Antone's promise on that."

She looked gravely at him across her shoulder.

"A pity more men around here haven't your balance and integrity, Reese."

"I don't know anything about that, Mary, but I do know I've got friends on both sides, and I don't want to see any of them hurt."

Canby ate hungrily of the swift meal Mary put together, and the food smoothed out some of the harshness in him. His after-meal cigarette tasted good. He got up and moved to the door.

"Someday I'll find a way to repay you for all your kindness to Sandy and me. It's your kind who've kept men civilized, Mary."

A hint of her old-time merriness came back. "Teach Sandy how to say those things, will you, Reese? Incidentally, Chris Lanifee was with me most of last night. You'll probably find her at the hotel."

Canby grinned. "Sight of Chris is always good for me. But right now I'm going to look at more unpleasant things."

Canby knew this country and its people. He knew that the news of the lynching would spread fast and that it would bring men to town to talk about it and to speculate on what it could develop into. He knew, too, that for any man to stay away from town too long would be considered almost a tacit admission of having had a hand in the thing. Clever men would realize this. On the other hand, men grown drunk and overbold with what they considered successful scheming and with their own importance might ride in and proclaim the act and dare opinion.

There was, mused Canby, no mystery about this thing. He was convinced that he could name at least some of the men who participated in the lynching. But proof was another thing. And some shade of proof he had to have, to bolster his own hand. When he and Newt Dyas had back-tracked that sign this morning, it was this proof they'd been after. Things hadn't worked out. Now he had to work other angles and wait for some shadow of that proof to appear. In the meantime, it would be smart to test public opinion pro and con. No better place to do this than the Desert House, where men gathered to drink and talk. So Canby angled up the street and pushed through the winnowing doors of the place.

Bert Lanifee was there. So were George Winter and Mason Garr. So was Cap Lovelock. So was Fox Baraby, of Starke and De Lacca's Tepee outfit.

Baraby stood a little apart from the others, his narrow face locked and inscrutable. He was toying now with an empty glass, which Tippo Vance did not seem to notice.

Bert Lanifee, George Winter, and Mason Garr all turned to Canby, and Lanifee said, "Chris told me about last night, Reese, and how you and Newt Dyas lit out. You've been to see Antone?"

"That's right, Bert."

"What's he going to do?"

"Prove himself a good citizen, as always. He's sitting tight."

"Damn!" exclaimed George Winter, "that's good news."

"Maybe," growled Mason Garr, "we've been afraid of ghosts. Antone must have lost all of the old fire."

"You're wrong there, Mason," said Canby bluntly. "It's just that Antone and his people are better men than some who would scheme out their ruin. I got Antone to sit tight on the promise that we'd clean up our own renegades."

"We?"

Canby looked the hard-bitten cattleman straight in the eye. "I expect to find a few men square enough to gag over a dirty, rotten, cowardly lynching of two innocent Apache boys. Damn it, Mason, what are you? It was proven to your face that Starke and De Lacca's first move against Ponco and Dobe was a cheap, lying frame-up. You backed their hand there and came out looking and feeling the fool. Are you going to back their hand in another dirtier deal?"

Fox Baraby said thinly, "Are you making accusations about that lynching, Canby?"

Canby looked at him, a hard, bright, entirely mirthless smile on his lips.

"Excuse me, gentlemen. This reminds me of something."

He moved straight in on Fox Baraby, who swung a little clear of the bar.

"Not too long ago, Baraby," said Canby, "you were ready to throw a gun on a decent man who was aiming to keep one of my boys from being mauled by a damn animal. Let's see you throw that gun on me!"

The whole room seemed to hang in suspended motion, then Mason Garr started to growl. Bert Lanifee silenced him with a hand that gripped Garr's arm savagely. Tippo Vance spoke calmly.

"He won't, Reese. There's a difference between throwing a gun on you than on me. Besides, he's alone."

Tippo was right. Fox Baraby snarled, but it was a cringing snarl. Reese Canby reached out a left hand and slapped Baraby across the face. Baraby's head rocked, and he backed up a stride. Canby followed him and slapped him again. He crowded Baraby back and back. He deliberately tramped on Baraby's toes. He slapped him twice more.

Sweat glistened on Fox Baraby's face, his teeth showing like those of a cornered rodent. His eyes were red with suffused hate. But he wouldn't draw.

Canby spat with contempt.

"Git, you damned coyote! And tell Chelso De Lacca I'm whittling a special club for him."

Half-drunk with helpless rage and shame, Fox

Baraby almost staggered to the door. Canby followed him, held the door open while he watched Baraby climb into his saddle, rowel his horse savagely, and explode away along the street.

"Sorry to run a customer away, Tippo," Canby said, coming back to the bar.

"No customer of mine," said Tippo. "Didn't see me pouring him any liquor, did you? Well, he's through drinking in this place. Him and the others, like Mike Partman and Milt Parrall."

Canby stopped dead still. "Milt Parrall?"

"Right! When your crew get down out of the Chevrons, ask who sent the word to them. Gentlemen, this one is on the house."

Mason Garr, staring at Tippo Vance, downed his drink almost automatically.

"You just said the damnedest thing, Tippo," he charged harshly. "I'm not sure I heard right. Did you say that Mike Partman and Milt Parrall can't drink here anymore?"

"That's right."

"Well, for God's sake! What are you trying to do, go broke?"

Tippo shrugged. "If I can't make a living serving those who, in my mind, shape up as men, why, then, yes—I'll go broke. Sometimes a man has to take a stand on things, Mason. This is my way of taking mine. It's my place and my liquor. I've a right to say who drinks in here and who doesn't. I hope you never make it necessary for me to include you in the black list."

"Tippo," exclaimed Cap Lovelock heartily, "you're quite a man. Damned if I ain't proud of you."

Mason Garr swung his head from side to side, almost like a bewildered bear. George Winter looked uneasy. There were drifts of current here that he couldn't read and slide along with. George Winter seldom saw anything but the obvious.

Bert Lanifee spoke slowly.

"Let's everybody keep his shirt on. And," he added significantly, "this might be a good time for every man to declare himself. Speaking for myself, I don't like that lynching business. I don't like any part of it. Reese, if you can hold Antone quiet through this, a lot of people will owe you a damn big debt."

Mason Garr found his voice in a bursting growl.

"Bert, set yourself one place or another. Where do you stand?"

"On my own feet," answered Lanifee calmly. "I've allowed myself to be led into one stupid spot. From here on in, I think for myself. You might be smart and do the same, Mason."

"I always think for myself," rapped Garr harshly. "And I do what I do because it suits me that way." He glared at Tippo Vance with angry eyes. "Tippo, if you ever refuse me a drink in this place, I'll come right over the bar after you."

Tippo met Garr's glare steadily. "The day you try it, you'll be dead before you get across. I'm through having anybody threaten me in my own place. Cut it fine, Mason!"

The door swung open, and Newt Dyas came in, moving up to the bar at Reese Canby's elbow. "Tepee ridin' in," he murmured. "Starke, De Lacca—the whole gang."

Canby nodded. "Thanks, Newt." He crooked a finger at Tippo Vance. "A quart, Tippo. Sealed."

Tippo was not the only one who was startled. Reese Canby was not a drinking man in any sense of the word. He took a casual one now and then with friends, but no more. George Winter, trying clumsily for humor, said, "For a sick friend, Reese?"

"Hardly a friend," Canby drawled.

Now came the clatter of hoofs in the street outside. Tippo Vance, setting the full sealed quart of liquor in front of Canby and scooping up the money Canby laid down, turned his head slightly, listening.

Spurs jangled and rasped, and then Sax Starke came in, followed by Chelso De Lacca, Al Sheeve, and others. At the tail of the line was Fox Baraby. Then, after the doors ceased to winnow, they swung inward again to let Mike Partman through.

Sax Starke spread a handful of change on the

bar. "Set 'em up, Tippo," he said. "I'm buying."

Tippo made no move to comply but ran a cold glance over the crowd. "Before we start," he said bluntly, "let's settle something once and for all. Baraby, don't drink over my bar anymore. Neither does Sheeve. Partman, I told you once how it was. I'm telling you once more for the final time. You don't drink in here again. I don't give a damn who you're with or who offers to buy. You don't drink! So, on your way. That takes in you, Baraby, and you, Sheeve. Get out and stay out!"

Sax Starke was plainly astounded. For a moment, all he could do was stare at Tippo. Then he exploded.

"What's that—*what's that?* You saying that some of my men can't drink here anymore, Vance? That Mike Partman can't?"

"That's right," retorted Tippo bluntly. "They can't."

"Why, you crazy damn fool—!"

"Easy, Sax," cut in Tippo. "In a minute you won't, either."

Chelso De Lacca, his broad, meaty face still showing plenty of the effect of Sandy Foss's fists, had been quiet, looking around. Now he spoke.

"So that's the way the cat jumps, eh? Well, it don't surprise me exactly. I been noticin' the signs lately."

Sax Starke scooped up the money he'd spread

and dropped it back in his pocket. "Any place my men can't drink, I don't drink. You're forgetting there's the Stag Head down the street a bit. We can do our drinkin' there from now on."

Tippo shrugged. "Fly to it. Your privilege. I'll get along."

Sax Starke's glance, running angrily along the bar, saw the full quart standing in front of Reese Canby. Starke's lips twisted.

"You sell it to some by the quart, yet you won't sell it to my men by the drink. Vance, I can take this damn place apart!"

Tippo reached under the bar, brought out a sawed-off shotgun, laid the gaping muzzle across the mahogany.

"Start in!"

Mason Garr growled, "Tippo, you don't know what you're doin'."

"I know exactly what I'm doin'," corrected Tippo. "I'm runnin' my place the way I want to run it. Them who don't like it don't need to stick around. Things goin' on across this range that I don't like. This is a good place and a good way to find out who's for the things that are right and who's for the things that are wrong."

"You figger you're qualified to judge such things?" put in Chelso De Lacca, mocking sarcasm in his moist, slippery voice. "Why, Tippo, you must be gettin' religion."

"Could be," said Tippo laconically. "One thing

is certain. I'm plenty fed up with you. So, startin' right now you don't drink here, either. I don't sell liquor to damn animals."

Thick as Chelso De Lacca's hide was, the words cut through it. Not so long ago, in this very same room, Sandy Foss had called him a slimy whelp. And now this, from Tippo Vance.

"Just for that, Vance," said De Lacca thickly, "I'm comin' around that bar and helpin' myself to a full quart. And let's see you try and stop me!"

To make good his threat, De Lacca had to pass Reese Canby, who stepped in front of him.

"You can have this quart, De Lacca," said Canby. "I bought it just for you. Take it—with Sandy Foss's compliments!"

Canby gripped the full quart by the neck and swung it—hard! It crashed down on De Lacca's head, shattered into fragments, the raw liquor cascading and splashing wildly. De Lacca went down like an axed hog.

Canby tossed the bottle neck aside. "Yeah," he said again, "for Sandy Foss—and what Sandy called you about. Next time, it'll be lead!"

Sax Starke swung away from the bar, but before he could do or say another thing, Tippo Vance banged the bar with his shotgun.

"This is loaded," he warned. "And I'm callin' the cards. Reese, I'm refundin' you the price of that quart. Never saw liquor used to better purpose. Starke, that thing on the floor belongs to you. Pick it up and take it out of here!"

Starke looked at Tippo. He looked at Reese Canby, at Newt Dyas, who stood still-faced and watchful at Canby's elbow. He looked at Cap Lovelock, who was grinning like an old war dog. He looked at Bert Lanifee, at Mason Garr, and at George Winter.

"All right," he said finally. "Right now, we'll find out something. Tepee is moving out of here—for good. From now on, you'll find us at the Stag Head. I'll buy the drinks over there." He stabbed a pointing finger at Mason Garr, at George Winter, and at Bert Lanifee. "You'll come drink with me?"

Bert Lanifee flushed at the tone and the words. "Don't throw orders at me, Sax. I drink where I please, and when."

"You're layin' somethin' on the line, Sax," growled Mason Garr. "When a man does that to me, I turn stubborn. If I feel like droppin' in at the Stag Head, I will. If I don't, I won't"

George Winter, uncertain as always, said nothing, but he stayed where he was.

"This," said Sax Starke savagely, "tells me what I want to know. I'll remember this when the ridin's done." He looked at Reese Canby again. "You," he gritted, "are finished. You'll find that out."

Canby smiled mirthlessly. "I'm lookin' for

five men, Starke. You could name them, but you won't. But I'll find the answer in my own way."

Tippo Vance rapped the bar again with his shotgun. "Get that thing off my floor!"

Sax Starke cursed, rapped out an order. Al Sheeve, Fox Baraby, and Mike Partman got hold of Chelso De Lacca, grunted and cursed as they heaved him erect and got shoulders under his arms. When they left with him, De Lacca's feet were dragging. He was still out. Sax Starke went with them.

Chapter VII
TANGLED TRAILS

Tippo Vance put his shotgun away. Cap Lovelock slapped the bar.

"This time I buy."

"Leave me out," said Mason Garr harshly. "Too much pushin' and haulin' goin' on. I'll drink any place I want, when I want. But I'll buy my own." He swung his head. "Canby, I didn't admire you just now. Chelso didn't even know what was comin'. No, I didn't like that."

Canby shrugged. "Do you know why Sandy Foss came in here and tackled De Lacca in the first place?"

"No, I don't. All I can say is that it was a damn-fool play on Foss's part. He should have known Chelso would take him apart. Yeah, Foss was a fool."

"Not in my book. He wouldn't be riding for me any more if he hadn't done just what he did. Sometimes, Mason, you talk before you know what you're talkin' about. Go find the answer and then see what you think."

The crusty cattleman threw both hands in the air, turned, and stamped out. George Winter hesitated a moment, then followed him. Bert

Lanifee leaned against the bar a little wearily.

"Once," he said, "this was a good range and a quiet one."

"One or two rotten spuds can raise hell with a barrel of good ones," observed Cap Lovelock. He added, almost plaintively, "I'd still like to buy that drink."

The Tepee crowd stayed in the Stag Head only long enough to get Chelso De Lacca reasonably on his feet again, then they rode out of town, De Lacca hunched low over his saddle horn, obviously a sick man.

From the doorway of Bob Stent's store Cap Lovelock watched them go. "Yes, sir, Bob," said Cap, rubbing his hands with satisfaction, "you never saw nobody knocked stiffer'n De Lacca was. Reese just hauled off with that full quart bottle and sure mashed De Lacca's ears back."

Bob Stent, as even-tempered, amiable, and fair-minded a man as ever walked, watched the receding riders with an ominously cold eye.

"If Chelso De Lacca ever puts foot in this store again, he goes out a dead man."

Mary Stent, starting to come into the store by the back way, heard both remarks. She hesitated, slipped quietly back to the kitchen, pensive and sober.

Milt Parrall rode into town, saw Chris Lanifee sitting on the hotel porch in Billy Eustace's favorite chair. He started to ride by, then, as though coming to some decision, spun his horse abruptly in to the rail and swung down. He pulled up a chair beside Chris.

"Comes a time, Chris," he said abruptly, "when a man has to know just where he stands."

Chris, startled, looked at him narrowly, then away. "Your tone," she said quietly, "hardly attracts me. Don't count on anything, Milt."

Parrall swung an impatient hand. "I got to know," he burst out, "one way or the other. Yes or no. Who is it? Me or Canby?"

Chris stiffened, color burning in her cheeks. "I don't know what you're talking about."

"You know very well what I'm talkin' about," insisted Parrall, almost roughly. "Me, I've dangled long enough. You know how I feel about you. I've shown it in a thousand ways and for a long time. You've never told me you didn't want me around. In fact, there's been plenty of times you've been pretty nice to me. Now, all of a sudden, in the past week or so, you've turned chilly on me. Who is it—Canby?"

Chris's eyes were dangerously bright. "Milt, you'd better change your tone and change the subject."

"No!" There was a moroseness in Milt Parrall, almost a sullenness. He leaned over and caught Chris by the arm. "You can't smile at a man, have him in your home, ride with him—and then start turning your back on him. Not when I'm that man. It's now or never. Which one? Canby or me?"

Chris jerked her arm away, stood up, blazing with anger. "You fool!" she cried. "It could never be you—now!"

With that, she turned on her heel and marched into the hotel, her back very straight.

Milt Parrall stared after her, his face twisted and working. He cursed, low and soundlessly. Rage leaped into his eyes. He got up, headed for the Desert House, drawn by long habit, then, recollecting, turned when but a stride or two from the door and went on to the Stag Head. There he began to drink.

Reese Canby and Newt Dyas, down in Pokey Carter's livery barn, currying and graining their horses, talked quietly back and forth.

"I don't rightly know where to start, Newt," said Canby. "I've made a promise to Anton I got to keep. If I should let him down, there's no telling what will happen. Using that promise as a lever, Antone will keep his young men quiet for a while. But when I talked with Antone last night, I could sense that he was old and tired and—well, not too sure how long he could keep the fires under control. I not only got to get results, I got to get them reasonably quick. You know and I know that Tepee pulled those lynchings. But we don't know the exact men who were in on it. I can't just barge in on Tepee and start shooting things up. Even if I made a job of it and came off with a whole hide, I'd forfeit a lot of backing that's just now beginning to come my way."

"Bert Lanifee, mebbe?" murmured Newt.

"That's right. And Judge Marland. Even Mason Garr and George Winter, though Winter's backing is just about as meaningless as his hostility."

"Mason Garr," said Newt flatly, "is a damned, ornery old vinegarroon!"

Canby smiled grimly. "But still a darned good man whose backing, or hostility, can mean a lot either way. Right now, Mason Garr is confused. He didn't like being suckered by Starke and De Lacca on that trumped-up cattle-stealing charge. But Mason is the sort that once he goes out on a limb, he hates to back off it. He's gagging over those lynchings. He's sore at Starke and De Lacca; he's sore at me. But mostly he's sore at himself. Given time, he'll come around."

"Mebbe." Newt shrugged. "I hope so. In the meantime, how do we go about making good on your promise to Antone?"

"I said I didn't know where to start, and I don't. But there's this one angle. Starke and De Lacca have tried twice to get Antone to jump over the traces, first on that false rustling deal, next with those lynchings. But Antone is still sitting tight. On its own, Tepee could never run the Apaches out of Sentinel Basin. To do that, Starke and De Lacca got to have backing. The only way they can get that backing is to force Antone to pick up the rifle again. That would set things off, awaken all the old hatreds and prejudices. So, failing in two tries, what will Starke and De Lacca do?"

"Make another try of some sort, I reckon."

"Exactly!" declared Canby. "In fact, they've got to. They can't afford to back down now. They've gone too far to stop. So I'm gambling that they'll make that third try, and a fourth and a fifth if they have to. What we got to do is catch them in the act."

"And how'll we go about doin' that?" Newt asked.

"Not by hanging around town. We're going to do a lot of prowling, Newt. We're going to be up early and stay out late. We're going to be watching every trail, reading every sign. You and me and Sandy Foss. We'll headquarter at my ranch, on the face of things. But we won't be around there much. We'll be riding."

"That makes sense." Newt nodded. "You want to draw a bead on a coyote, you got to be out where he's prowlin'. When do we start?"

"Tonight, if it looks like Sandy can sit a saddle. He took a tough lickin', but he's the sort to bounce back fast."

Newt chuckled in his thin, dry way. "Chelso De Lacca won't bounce back. If he ain't got an inch-wide crack in his skull, it's because it's solid bone from ear to ear. You realize how hard you hit him, Reese?"

"I did my best to cave his damn skull in," declared Canby harshly. "If the bottle hadn't quit, maybe I would have."

"After all this big talk and swagger, you'd have thought Sax Starke would have gone on the warpath then and there," suggested Newt. "De Lacca will probably remind him of that later."

"I thought of that," admitted Canby. "Of course, there was you and me and Cap Lovelock. And Tippo with his shotgun. And Bert Lanifee and Mason Garr are not nearly as ready to pick up a war belt for him as they were a few weeks ago, especially Bert. Such things make a difference."

The day ran its slow, hot course. Reese Canby, watching his chance, went back to the Desert House when he could catch Tippo Vance alone.

"Tippo," he said, "what about Milt Parrall?"

Tippo considered carefully. "You asked him to get that word to your crew up in the Chevrons. You wanted it done right away, pronto! After you left, I waited for him to get about it. He didn't. He started playing solitaire. Finally, I asked him was he or wasn't he going to. He made some remark about you always being in a hurry. Right then, I got my first real look at Milt Parrall. He wasn't going to send that word for you, or, if he did, not with the hurry up he'd let you figger he would. So I told him to get the hell out of my place and never come back, that I'd send the word myself. And I did."

"Who'd you send?"

"Danny Potter. He'd got in an argument with Mason Garr, and either he quit or Garr fired him, I don't know which. Anyway, I slipped him ten bucks and told him to get traveling. He lit right out."

Canby put ten dollars on the bar and pushed it across. "Thanks, Tippo. Thanks for a lot of things. If everybody had the nerve to take the kind of stand you have, we'd have a quiet range around here."

Tippo shrugged. "Right's right and wrong's wrong, Reese. Apaches got rights, same as anybody else. And I don't like slickery gents, no matter what color shirt they got on. You figgered Parrall a pretty good friend, didn't you?"

"I did," admitted Canby gravely.

He went out and saw Milt Parrall's horse tied over in front of the hotel. He also saw Bert and Chris Lanifee getting ready to leave town. He went over there.

Bert seemed grim, a little dour, and Chris plainly had something on her mind. Canby stood beside the buckboard, looking up at them. "Thanks, Bert," he said.

Bert, startled, growled, "What for?"

"This and that. I knew you'd get your back up. Chris, we'll finish that talk one of these days, the one we were having when the news of the lynching came in."

Chris flushed. "Perhaps."

Bert shook the reins, and the buckboard scudded away. Canby stared after it, frowning. "Now what the devil," he muttered, "has got into Chris? She's upset over something."

He went into the hotel and asked Billy Eustace if he knew where Milt Parrall was. Billy said he didn't. Billy was getting the mail ready for the stage. Canby went out and sat on the porch with the hotel-keeper, awaiting the stage's arrival.

Billy said, "Some folks are changin' their minds, Reese—about this and that."

"Meaning?"

"Nobody likes being made a sucker of," said Billy obliquely. "That cattle-rustling charge turned up as such a shoddy, lying deal. You stick something like that down the throats of good men, and they're goin' to gag, regardless of past prejudices."

"No joke about those lynchings, Billy," said Canby soberly.

The hotel-keeper looked at him shrewdly. "You aim to do something about that, boy?"

"I got to. I made a promise to Antone. And you don't break your given word to an Apache, Billy, because hell and torture couldn't make them break theirs."

"That's true," admitted Billy, rocking a little faster. "Well, you keep your ears and eyes open, and you'll pick up a trail. Sax Starke's the sort to get clumsy when he gets mad. And he's plenty mad about now. I'd like to have been there when you wasted a quart of good liquor on Chelso De Lacca's skull. Now there's a first-rate side-winder for you."

The stage rolled in, made its pause, then went on again, sucking the dust along. Sundown spread its crimson across the desert, and the Pahvant Rim lost its sultry fire as the first blue shadows began to climb and flow.

Reese Canby headed for Bob Stent's store, wondering what Mary Stent would have to say about him getting Sandy Foss into the saddle again. He was passing the Stag Head when Milt Parrall came out, weaving a little. Canby spoke quietly.

"Milt!"

Parrall paused, feet spread, the breath of too much liquor strong off him. Canby had never seen Parrall this way before. He dropped a hand on Parrall's arm.

"Something's getting away from you and me, old-timer, that's too valuable to lose. Let's talk this over and get squared away again."

Parrall stared through liquor-bleared eyes, jerked his arm free.

"Keep your hands off me," he snarled thickly. "I want no part of you. I'm plenty fed up with these self-appointed saviors of the rights of men and all that damned hogwash. Get away from me!"

"We'll put that down to the liquor in you, Milt—and try again," Canby said patiently.

"Liquor be damned!" blurted Parrall. "Drunk or sober, I know when I've had enough of you."

He would have gone on, but Canby caught his arm once more.

"No! That may satisfy you, but it doesn't me. What's got into you, anyhow?"

Parrall cursed, aimed a clumsy blow at Canby, missed, then fumbled for his gun. Canby slammed him against the front of the Stag Head, held him there, and took his gun away from him.

"Now," he rapped grimly, "we'll get down to cases. There's a reason for this. What is it?"

Milt Parrall seemed to sag a little, then caught himself, stared back into Canby's eyes. "It could be," he said with a slow, labored distinctness, "that I hate your guts!"

Bunched muscles knotted and crawled along the angle of Canby's jaw.

"You're sober enough to know what you're saying. Sure of that?"

"Yeah," said Parrall. "I'm sure of it—damned sure!"

Canby stared at him a moment longer, stepped

back, and handed him his gun. He spoke almost gently.

"If you ever change your mind, Milt, I'd like to hear of it. Because I'm leaving the door open. Good luck!"

He turned away and went on, a tall, broad shape in the dusk. Parrall swung his head, watching him go. Once he half lifted the gun, but there was no real decision in the move. He dropped the weapon back into its holster, cursed blindly, spun around, and went lurching back into the Stag Head.

A gray bitterness lurked deep in Canby's eyes when he entered the Stent living quarters by the back way, but he smiled at Mary.

"Gather yourself an armful of pots and pans and get ready to start throwing them, Mary," he said, "because I'm taking Sandy away from your gentle care."

His smile did not fool this girl; she glimpsed what lay in his eyes.

"I won't object, Reese, if you think it necessary," she said simply.

"It's necessary. The feeling is strong in me that I've been wasting time. I've been letting little things hide the big ones. And I really think Sandy can stand some saddle leather under him again. He'll damn me, of course, for taking him away from you."

"No, he won't," corrected Mary. "He's in

a terrible stew to be up and around again."

Sandy proved exultant. "Anything to get out of this cussed bed," he declared. "Not," he added hastily, with a guilty look at Mary, "that it ain't one swell bed and the surroundin's plumb wonderful. But a man was intended to be up an' doin', not layin' around like a useless rag doll. Mebbe I look kinda frayed out, but I'm really plenty chipper. Reese, what's this I hear about you chunkin' De Lacca with a whisky bottle?"

"Seems I recall you advising a club instead of fists on that hombre," Canby drawled. "Well, at the moment that whisky bottle was the best club I could find."

"Cap Lovelock says you really flattened De Lacca," Sandy said eagerly. "I'd sure like to have seen that."

"The bottle turned out to be a little bit harder than De Lacca's head," admitted Canby. "Now let's see if you can get into your clothes and stagger around."

By the time Sandy, grunting and squirming and with Canby's help, got into his clothes, Mary had supper going. Bob Stent came in from the store, considerably grimmer than his usual amiable self. He said simply, "You boys are all right. Anything you do with De Lacca and Starke meets with my complete approval."

Supper over with, Canby and Sandy prepared to leave. Mary, getting Canby alone for a moment, murmured, “I’m sorry to be such a care, Reese. Maybe—maybe I was imagining things.”

Canby shook his head. “Sooner or later, the off strain in a mongrel always shows up, Mary. Any woman has a right to live and move through the world without a whelp like De Lacca making things unpleasant for her. So just you forget the whole thing and get the old merry smile back.”

Later that evening, just about the time Bob Stent was going to close up, Mason Garr came stamping into the store.

“I ain’t the nosy sort,” said Garr abruptly, “but when all manner of things are in the air, and anything’s liable to break at any time, a man likes to know the why and wherefore. There’s this I’m wonderin’ about. First, it’s young Foss tangling with Chelso De Lacca and taking a first-class licking. Then today I see Reese Canby, with hardly a lick of warnin’, club De Lacca down like he would a mad dog. You know why, Bob?”

“Yes.” Stent nodded. “I know why. So does my girl, Mary. Right here in this store, she had to throw my gun on De Lacca to make him mind his manners. With that same gun, I’ll kill De Lacca if he ever sets foot in this store again. That answer your question?”

Mason Garr stood, scowling, pinching his lower lip between thumb and forefinger. He jerked his head almost violently. “Yeah, that answers it. Thanks.”

Without another word, Mason Garr turned and walked out.

Out at Reese Canby's Diamond R C, Sandy Foss, Newt Dyas, and Reese Canby made their preparations. The ride out from town had done Sandy a lot of good, loosening up and smoothing out muscles that had been knotted and stiff from the beating and inaction. His face was still a long way from normal, but he wasn't minding that.

"We'll grab a little sleep and then get away real early," said Canby. "Come daylight, we'll be sifting the rims and the hills."

That was the way it was. From a point not far from the spot where Dobe and Ponco had been lynched, Canby, Sandy, and Newt Dyas watched the rose and pearl-gray dawn spill over the eastern edge of the world and dilute the black shadows of night. Sentinel Basin was a vast cauldron of thin boiling mists. Somewhere down there, a cow bawled faintly, greeting the day. A little wind played back and forth, caught between day and night, and uncertain which way to turn.

"You'll stick pretty close to here, Sandy," ordered Canby. "Keep your eyes and ears open and don't advertise yourself by ramming around too careless. Just remember that this was a rough game right from the start, and that it'll get rougher before it's done. Don't," he ended dryly, "spit in the devil's eye, because from here on in fists are forgotten weapons. If Newt and I don't show up before sundown, you drift back to Warden Spring. We'll meet you there."

Where Sandy was stationed was due west of the heart of Sentinel Basin. Newt Dyas drifted south from there to keep an eye on the southwest curve of the basin, while Canby rode wide and circled onto the north rim. East lay the Apache rancheria, well guarding all that side of the basin. So now it would be a game of patience and watchful waiting.

There was a point where the rocks bunched up, some of them higher than a mounted man's head. In a pocket among these, where the animal would be hidden from any casual survey, Canby left his horse. For himself, he selected a forward spot where, sitting, he could rest the broad of his shoulders against a rock face. He built a smoke and watched the day boil up across the basin. He pulled his hat low and squinted his eyes into the blaze of the new sun. Night's coolness evaporated instantly when the sun touched it. These rocks, Canby mused, would be an oven within an hour, and to make the day endurable, he'd have to move out and go higher, up where the piñon forest began.

He wasn't at all sure that this new maneuver of his would bring results. Maybe the course of action he'd figured Sax Starke and Chelso De Lacca would take was too obvious. Maybe sensing the turn of opinion in men whose backing they had counted on would make the Tepee owners cautious, perhaps even cause them to discard their original idea entirely. In which case, there would be a lot of uneasy waiting and watching ahead, until Starke and De Lacca came up with some new angle.

Of one thing he felt reasonably positive. Sax Starke was a man driven by a sort of perverse ambition. Sax Starke had to be big. He was the sort to judge all things by extent, rather than capacity. It was in him to yearn ceaselessly to be top dog, to dominate. And all history, mused Canby grimly, was full of catastrophes brought about by such perverse ambitions in men.

The extent of the Tepee range was already wide, but it wasn't too good a range, its capacity for steady grazing definitely limited. Handled shrewdly, it was enough to satisfy any normal man. But Starke and De Lacca had not handled it shrewdly. They had poured more cattle onto it than it could sustain, so it was overgrazed. Rather than cut down the size of their herd, Starke and De Lacca had turned in the other direction. They wanted more grass. That grass lay in Sentinel Basin, if they could get it.

Starke's ambition was like a compressed spring, constantly pressing outward. North, west, and south, in a rough half circle, the ranges of Mason Garr, George Winter, Milt Parrall, Bert Lanifee, and of Canby himself contained that pressure.

Any attempt to expand in these directions would have brought the massed anger of all these cattlemen down on Tepee's head, and Tepee could not stand up under this. So the pressure, unless controlled, would have to move east. And east lay Sentinel Basin. East lay Apache land.

Canby shook his head with somber impatience. That was the hell of such ambitions. Generally, men like Sax Starke ended up destroying themselves, but they always sucked other men into the vortex with them; they left so many of the innocent maimed or dead behind them. Already, across this range, the poison had begun to spread. Already, there had been dead men and friendships strained or broken.

Canby thought of Milt Parrall, and that thought hurt. It hurt all the more because he could not understand what had gotten into Parrall. Reese Canby had felt that he could bet on Milt Parrall anywhere, any time, and now found that he couldn't. Drunk, but not that drunk, Milt Parrall had cursed him, said that he hated his guts. Just like that. Like a slap in the face. Why?

Try as he would, Canby could think of no single thing he had ever done to bring about such a change. It was, he mused bleakly, tough to have an accepted, long-time friend turn on you so bitterly and abruptly and for no discernible reason. A thing like that shook a man up, knocked all sense of the sureness of things out of him, left him wondering and uncertain.

True, Milt Parrall had never been a demonstrative sort. There was a lot of silence in Milt, which at times verged on the moody. But there had been plenty of times in the past when he and Milt had spent rollicking times together, found laughter and a carefree companionship. But now a change had come, a change dating from Sax Starke's and Chelso De Lacca's opening move for expansion and power.

In those moments in town, in front of the Stag Head, Milt Parrall's words had been freighted with bitterness, even hatred, and his moves openly hostile. Milt had never been a drunkard. For all this, as Canby saw it, only Sax Starke and Chelso De Lacca could be blamed. Sax Starke and Chelso De Lacca.

Chelso De Lacca. That sly, slimy, hulking brute, with his moist words and fleshy laughter. Well, he wouldn't be laughing now. He'd be nursing a clubbed head and building up more treacherous hate. Canby stirred restlessly at the thought. The dirty whelp! Annoying a girl like Mary Stent.

Well, the incident proved one thing. It proved the correctness of Canby's first instinctive judgment of De Lacca. Here was a man who moved on a different plane than other men. He had a trail all of his own, down in the shadows, where things were dank and reptilian. He was something out of the ooze, was Chelso De Lacca.

Movement down in the basin jerked Reese Canby out of his burden of thought. Apache herdsmen, working stock. The distance was considerable, which made the riders and cattle Lilliputian figures. Gradually, the riders worked closer, and now Canby could see what they were about: they were turning cattle away from this western part of the basin and pushing them east.

Here it was again—proof of old Antone's wisdom and long-suffering steadfastness to the principles of peace. Antone knew that the west rim of Sentinel Basin was the danger area. By keeping the tribal herd away from it, he was lessening the chance of further incident that might stir up red wrath and carnage across this world. He had made a promise; he had taken one. Antone was leaving nothing to chance. He would keep his promise.

Those Apache riders were good hands with cattle. They were superb in the saddle. They were of a race that had been harried from pillar to post, dispossessed time and again, betrayed by the unscrupulous, damned and cursed because they had, in the old days, fought fiercely to retain possession of an empire that had been theirs centuries before the first white man had ever put foot on the continent.

Broken and scattered, helpless before a tide of power they could not match, they had, with stoic fatalism, accepted the inevitable. They had seized upon what small opportunity the future had to offer them as a people, worked with fanatical zeal, and built this small fabric of independence for themselves in a land theoretically dedicated to that principle. It was, mused Reese Canby, a principle that Sax Starke and Chelso De Lacca had apparently never heard about.

Some of the cattle, stirred up by the activity deeper in the basin, began drifting up the slope toward the west rim. A couple of Apache riders swung a fast circle, aiming to come in above the cattle and head them off. The maneuver brought the two riders to within a short five hundred yards of where Reese Canby sat. And it was when they were at the nearest spot of their approach that, off to Canby's left, the thin, hard, ringing crash of a rifle shattered the hot silence of the morning.

Watching the two Apache riders, Canby saw the spurt of dust where the rifle slug struck just short of them. Even as Canby lunged to his feet, that rifle crashed again. At this shot, the horse of the leading rider humped up, made two or three stiff-legged jumps, then piled up, its rider swinging clear just before it collapsed.

The second rider sped up beside his unhorsed comrade who, running along beside for a few strides, swung up behind. Then, carrying double, the second horse raced away down slope. Three more rifle shots slashed after them, but the range, long in the first place, grew swiftly excessive, and the shooting stopped.

By this time, Canby had dodged back through the rocks to where his horse stood. He yanked his rifle from the saddle scabbard, darted into the open past the screen of rocks. Out there, on another rocky point some three hundred yards away, a man was crouched, rifle in hand. He had been staring down into the basin, watching the fleeing Apache riders. But the movement of Canby coming into the open caught his eye, and he swung swiftly around, rifle leaping to his shoulder.

Canby got there with the first shot. It was at best a chancy one, a snap-shot at a distance far from certain, yet it brought abrupt results. Canby saw his man lurch and spin, saw him drop his rifle, clattering off the rocks. Then the fellow made a jump that carried him out of sight.

Canby slammed two more shots against the rocks and ran back for his horse. By the time he was in the saddle and moving into the clear, another horse had already burst into the open off the far point and was racing away, heading high, toward the piñon forest. Its rider was crouched low, one arm swinging loosely, spurring frantically.

Canby tried a shot, missed, and was about to try another when he realized it was useless business. For with his own horse, half-spooked and edgy under him, dancing and sidling and with the target scudding and dodging and lengthening the range with every jump, a hit now was a thousand-to-one chance. There was only one sound course: to run the fellow down. Canby set about doing it.

In this first stage of the race, Canby gained little if any ground. His quarry reached the first ragged fringe of the piñons and was a flash of movement among them, then disappeared into the thicker growth. By the time Canby raced into these trees, blue-green at close hand, but shading almost to blackness with distance, the world was empty and silent.

Canby slowed his racing mount. This would take headwork as well as speed. One thing was in his favor. Here in the piñons, the ground was soft enough to leave plain sign. Even a horse at a walk must leave a trail behind it, while a running one gouged deep marks.

Canby followed the sign at a trot, weaving and dodging through the timber. The way led straight north for a time. Eventually, it would lead a man around the east end of the Chevrons, through a country vast and empty and with no trails or human habitation within fifty miles. It was no way for a sound man to flee, let alone a wounded one, for Canby knew he'd got lead into the fellow with that first shot. The dropped rifle and loose-hanging arm told that. Sheer panic or a desperate attempt to mix up his trail and so shake pursuit were all that could keep the quarry heading north.

In sudden decision, Canby swung his horse toward the west. He was making a guess at this, gambling that in time his quarry would turn west, too, hoping to circle back to lower range, where shelter and aid for that wounded arm could be had. With luck, Canby figured, he might intercept this move.

To have followed the sign of the fleeing horse would have kept Canby on the sure trail as long as the rider kept to the piñon forest, but this did not mean too much of a chance for capture. For one thing, the fellow could flee faster than Canby could follow, and, for another, once he turned back and down, got safely into the lower country, he could lose his sign on some stretch of cap rock, or at least slow Canby up to a point where his complete getaway would be comparatively easy. No, this was a time to think and gamble.

As he rode, Canby fixed his mind on the country ahead. This westerly direction would, in time, bring a man into the brakes above Telescope Creek and Canby's own ranch headquarters. The quarry would have to turn south at this point or before or would find himself beyond the junction of the northern end of Pahvant Rim and the lower shoulders of the Chevrons. Once beyond that point, there was no way down to the desert and the black sage range except by the rim trail just above the town of Cassadora. Canby doubted the fellow would want to chance this, for it would mean advertising that wounded arm to some sharp-eyed citizen in town. If the quarry turned down, it would be somewhere between here and Telescope Creek. Satisfied with that conclusion, Canby acted on it.

He worked down slope to his left at a long slant, until the scattering of the piñons advertised he was nearing the outer fringe of them. And along here, where he had a fair view of both ahead and to the rear, and clear view of the open country below, he rode slowly, rifle ready across his saddle, alertness holding him tall and straight in the saddle.

This was a country of sloping ridges, springing from the main flank of the piñon hills, flowing down and losing themselves finally in the lower flats. Between the ridges ran gulches, and Canby dipped in and out of these, his horse grunting and scrambling with exertion. On each ridge top, Canby would rein in to look and listen before going on.

The heat of the day was building up. Sweat darkened the horse's hide around the edges of the saddle blanket. It built up under the band of Canby's hat, trickled down his face; on the backs of his hands, it made a faint beading.

Carrying down from the higher slope came the dismal croaking of a startled raven. Canby's horse, just topping the backbone of another of the down-slanting ridges, slid back a stride, so swiftly did Canby rein in. Canby's swinging glance picked up the raven, lifting and circling, then winging away, its raucous protest thinning and dying out.

Canby waited, taut with alertness. Now came the muffled crack of a deadfall broken through, then the thud of running hoofs. Canby drove forward past another gulch to another ridge top and saw a rider sift through the piñon fringe and break into the open on the next ridge ahead.

It was Jack Naile, and he was blind sick and reeling in his saddle, all the left shoulder and sleeve of his shirt soggy dark with blood. Canby whipped his rifle to his shoulder, then lowered it again, for it was obvious that Naile could not stick his saddle much longer. He hunched lower and lower in his saddle as his horse tipped past a shoulder of the ridge and went plunging on down slope.

Canby raced after him, angling across the intervening gulch, storming after a horse that carried a rider, but which was now running without command or direction. Naile lay farther and farther out along the neck of his horse, face buried in the whipping mane, both arms hanging and swaying loosely.

The fleeing horse swung sharply, taking advantage of a more favorable swing of the slope. This abrupt change of direction did what Canby figured it would. Jack Naile rolled loosely from his saddle and piled up, looking like a dead man as Canby roared past, intent on the capture of Naile's horse.

A quarter of a mile below, Canby cornered the animal against the slope. He led it back to where Naile lay, out but not dead, blood welling in clotted crimson from the wound in his shoulder. Unconsciousness in no way improved Jack Naile's expression. His narrow features were pulled into a taut, set snarl. Canby straightened him out, pulled off his neckerchief, and fashioned a rough bandage for Naile's wound.

Chapter VIII
THE OMINOUS TIDE

Mason Garr was a deeply troubled man. He had spent the night in Billy Eustace's hotel and now, in the bright, hot pour of a new day, stood on the porch of the hotel and tried to make up his mind. A hard-working man all his life, he was devoted to the welfare of his ranch, which took in all the southern swing of the black sage country. The feeling was nagging at him now that he should be out there, deep in the usual routine of things, guiding the daily run of ranch affairs. But there was an even stronger feeling holding him here in town.

Thunder was growling across this country, its note deepening and growing more ominous with every passing day. Battle lines were forming, men's opinions jelling, growing more solid by the hour. It was increasingly plain that lasting future judgment of every man would depend on where he took his stand now.

In the beginning, it had not been so difficult. Aside from one or two fiery individualists about town, men like Billy Eustace and Cap Lovelock, mass opinion had been pretty much the same. The cattle-stealing charge against Ponco and

Dobe, the two Apache riders, was being handled through accepted channels of law. It had been easy to let the old hatreds and suspicions stifle any thin doubts a man might have held regarding the soundness of the charge brought against these two Indians; it had been reasonably natural that a man stick to his own kind in a case like that.

There had been plenty of substantial company to help brush away any small whisperings of conscience. Even Bob Stent, whose fairness of mind no man could ever question, had spoken no real protest against that trial. Things had seemed fairly settled and right until that young Reese Canby had ridden in to upset the bean pot, to prove the whole thing a shabby farce, a lie, a piece of rank injustice. And to show up those who had followed the lead of Sax Starke and Chelso De Lacca as either gullible fools or greedy, callous schemers.

Mason Garr, sucking grimly on a pipe that had clogged up, hammered the bowl of it angrily against a porch post. If he looked at himself fairly, how much of his own gullibility in the affair had been due to being a plain damn fool? How much to the stirrings of greed? Yeah, how much to the lure of a chunk of Sentinel Basin grass?

Mason Garr had prided himself on his judgment of men. His friendship, like his enmity, he gave slowly. But once given, they stood. Only one thing could make him change—a sellout, a double-cross.

This gruff, hard-bitten cattleman had his own code of ethics. In the main, it was a good code. Perhaps the strongest part of that code was a complete respect for a good woman. This, in Mason Garr's eyes, should be as fundamental in any man as breathing, requiring no more conscious effort.

So it was that while he might have overlooked the unfair trial of Dobe and Ponco and while, though it had shaken and upset him, he might even have found some kind of excuse for the later lynching of these two, the thing that Bob Stent had told him concerning Chelso De Lacca had set fire to a deep and bitter wrath.

Mason Garr, a bachelor, had never known a family of his own. Down the years, he had watched Mary Stent grow up from a sturdy, happy youngster to an attractive, smiling young lady. She had always been a favorite of Mason Garr's. Her presence in her father's store had always made it a fine place for a crusty, gruff, but often lonely cattleman to visit and while away an hour. Lacking a daughter of his own, Mason Garr had known a deep, quiet, unspoken affection for this girl.

And, though he had never hinted of his feelings in any way, there were times when he felt that this dark-eyed, black-haired girl understood his feelings and in small, gentle ways had shown a return of his affection. Which had delighted him and sent him away warmly content.

But she'd had to take a gun to keep Chelso De Lacca in his place!

Mason Garr cursed, softly but harshly.

"Don't let me interfere, Mason," said Billy Eustace from behind him. "Go ahead. You got yourself out in the open now. Take a good look at yourself. Does any man good, every now and then, to take lye soap an' a stiff-bristled scrubbin' brush to what he may call his soul."

The old rocking chair creaked as Billy lowered himself into it.

Mason Garr turned on him. "You," he growled, "jump to conclusions too much."

"Not jumping now," retorted Eustace calmly. "I sit here in this old chair of mine. I watch men ride up and down the street. I see 'em show some wisdom an' a lot of damn foolishness. You watch a hillside long enough, Mason, an' you get plumb familiar with the sunshine an' the shadow on it."

"What kind of talk is that?"

"My kind. It makes sense to me." Billy Eustace smiled faintly. "Mebbe I'm a philosopher."

Hoofs chunked at the head of the street. It was Sax Starke, Fax Baraby, and Al Sheeve. As they passed the hotel, Sax Starke swung his horse's head and reined in. Baraby and Sheeve went on down to the Stag Head.

"Want to talk with you, Mason," called Starke.

"And I with you," growled Garr. "Where's De Lacca?"

"Out at the ranch. Why?"

"Tell him to stay away from me. Tell him to stay plumb away from me!"

"That's what I wanted to talk to you about," said Starke. "Chelso's sorry about that. He'd been drinking too much and—"

"Liquor be damned!" exploded Mason Garr. "He's a slimy whelp. You can tell him I said so. I wish that bottle Reese Canby used on him had been iron instead of glass. You'll get rid of De Lacca, Starke, or you'll be touched with the same smell."

Swift anger flamed in Starke's eyes. A retort formed on his lips, but he held it back. He gigged his horse sharply and went on to the Stag Head at a run.

Billy Eustace chuckled softly. "You can forget the lye an' the scrubbin' brush, Mason. You're plumb clean inside now." Billy folded his hands across his stomach. "I feel good—good!"

Mason Garr pulled up a chair and sat down. He was silent while he dug the dottle from his pipe with his pocketknife, got a refill of tobacco, and puffed freely. Then he spoke gruffly.

"Feel better myself."

The heat of the day was building up, and the town moved languidly. Mike Partman came down past the courthouse, turned in at the Stag Head. Mason Garr watched him with a scowling glance.

"We need a new sheriff, Billy," he said abruptly. "Star looks outta place on a damned worm."

Billy Eustace's musing smile broadened. "Mason, you amaze me. But I like the change. Next thing I know, you'll be ridin' out to visit Antone and smoke the pipe of peace."

"Not me," declaimed Garr hastily. "I got no use for an Apache, an' never will have."

A figure came out of Pokey Carter's livery barn, slouched and slow-moving. It was Milt Parrall. He was disheveled, his eyes bloodshot and bleary. Particles of straw clung to him. He looked like a man who had slept off a drunk in Pokey Carter's hayloft. Which was what he was.

He came up the street, crossed to the Stag Head, close enough for Mason Garr and Billy Eustace to read his condition. Garr stirred restlessly.

"I never saw him that way before. What the devil's got into the man anyhow?"

"When," answered Billy Eustace quietly, "a man like Milt gets himself in that shape, it means he's either lost faith in the world or in himself. With Milt, I figure it's the last. He took a good look at himself and saw somethin' he tried to blot out with an overload of whisky. Now that he's soberin' up again, he'll either be a better man than he ever was or one a durned sight worse."

Mason Garr made a pounding movement with

a clenched fist, a characteristic gesture when he was upset.

"What the devil's gone wrong with this country?" he burst out. "A few weeks ago, it was the same good country we'd known for so many years. You could reach out a finger an' put it on any man at any time, because you knew just where he stood. Now you can't put a finger on anybody."

"Yes, you can," corrected Billy Eustace softly. "There are some who are just where they always were, Mason. It's only the shifty ones who keep skittering around so you can't place 'em."

Mason Garr slouched deeper in his chair, puffing morosely.

A buckboard came skirling in, chased by a sweep of dust that was a slow-drifting amber haze in the still air.

"Bert and Chris Lanifee," grunted Garr. "Ain't anybody goin' to stay home and tend to the chore of raisin' cows? Way Bert spoke yesterday, he was goin' to do just that from now on. Yet here he is again."

"Tides runnin' across the range, Mason," said Billy Eustace. "Got thunder an' lightnin' an' sudden death in 'em. Folks realize that. They're restless." Billy got up out of his chair. "Mornin', Bert—Chris."

Chris got down and came up on the porch. Bert stayed at the reins. "Guess you think I'm a locoed fool, Billy," he said ruefully, "but Sis and me'll headquarter with you for a while. There's nothing out at the ranch—but the ranch."

Billy Eustace nodded. "I understand, Bert. Glad you brought Chris. She brightens up this old hotel of mine. Like a bunch of fresh wildflowers in the parlor."

Chris colored slightly, smiled, but her eyes were grave. "With you," she said, "we feel we're with a friend, Billy. And friends have come to mean more and more. Mr. Garr, how are you?"

Mason Garr made a surprising reply. "I'm an old, befuddled fool, lass. And plumb happy to have you and Bert around. It comes to me that I been livin' wrong for too many years. Livin' with myself, I've become ingrown and crotchety and stupid. You folks look good to me. Stay close around. I'm buyin' your dinner."

Chris dropped a slim hand on the old cattleman's shoulder. "Invitation accepted, with thanks."

Bert Lanifee looked startled. "Mason," he said, "is that you?"

Billy Eustace chuckled. "Mason's been doin' a chore of housecleanin'. He likes the result. Makes him feel young and coltish."

Bert Lanifee swung the buckboard around and drove down to the livery barn. He was still there when Reese Canby came riding into town along the Reservation Road, leading a horse carrying

Jack Naile, who was hunched low in his saddle. His wrists were tied to the saddle horn, his ankles to the cinch rings. He was bloody and haggard and teetering on the rim of unconsciousness.

Canby spied the group on the hotel porch and reined down that way. His face was bleak, but his eyes warmed slightly at the sight of Chris Lanifee. He touched his hat to her but spoke to Billy Eustace.

"See if you can round up Doc Snell and Mike Partman, will you, Billy? Send 'em both over to the jail."

The hotel-keeper nodded, but before he could move, Mason Garr growled, "What you got there, Canby?"

"Something that shouldn't be allowed to run loose in the hills. Something that needs to be locked up and sewed up."

Mason Garr went down the steps. "I'll get Partman."

The jail was empty and open. Reese Canby untied Jack Naile, hauled him from the saddle, and had to half carry him in and lay him out on a bunk. Mason Garr came in with Mike Partman.

"What the devil is this, Canby?" demanded the sheriff angrily. "There's no place in my jail for a wounded man."

"There is for this one," answered Canby crisply. "He'll live or die here just as well as anywhere. But while he lives, he stays here, locked up.

Get that clear, Partman. He stays, locked up!"

"Be damned if he does!" cried Partman furiously. "Not without my say-so. What right you got to bring a man in and tell me I got to lock him up? How'd he get that bullet note in him? Who shot him, and why? There's a lot of questions to be answered, Canby. Suppose you start answering some of them."

"Mike," said Mason Garr bluntly, "you've turned out to be damned poor color. Shut up and do as you're told, or I make it my personal chore to strip that star off you and run you plumb outta the country. Soon as Doc Snell shows and does what he can, you lock Naile in here and keep him locked until you're told different. Notice you bounce when Sax Starke barks. Well, somebody else is barkin' now, but you bounce anyway."

Doc Snell came hurrying in. He asked no questions, just got to work. He needed hot water, and Mason Garr went after some. When he returned, Bert Lanifee and Bob Stent were following him. And presently Sax Starke came in.

Starke's eyes were cold, his expression locked. He crowded up and looked down at Jack Naile who, at the first touch of Doc Snell's probe, had sighed deeply and slid into unconsciousness again. Doc spoke curtly. "No need for half the town crowding around. I can handle this alone now."

They went out into the sheriff's office, Starke still with that locked expression, saying nothing.

"I can't help but be curious," said Bert Lanifee. "What happened?"

Reese Canby spun a smoke before speaking, then he told the story with curt emphasis. "It was as cold-blooded an attempt at dry-gulching as I ever saw," he ended. "Had the range been a little shorter, there would have been a couple of Apache riders dead out there in the basin instead of just an Apache horse. Had there been, then no power on earth could have kept the Mescaleros in line, not even Antone's authority. And nobody could legitimately blame them. Starke, you're walkin' on damn thin ice."

Sax Starke flushed. "I had nothing to do with the affair. For that matter, how do we know you're giving us this straight?"

"Yeah," parroted Mike Partman, "how do we know you're givin' us the real story, Canby?"

Canby took a deep inhale, spun the cigarette aside, took two quick steps, and locked a taut fist in Partman's shirt front. He jammed Partman against the wall, poured a blaze of bleak anger on the startled, shrugging sheriff.

"Mike," he gritted, "I've had just about all I can stand from you. I gave you a chance to do something about that dry-gulch attempt on me. You haven't even bothered to speak to me about it since. You just haven't given a damn. Or maybe you sort of approve of that sort of thing. Mike, you're nothing but a booze-lapping, rotten excuse for a sheriff. Don't ever suggest I'm lying about anything again, or I'll slap your ears off, sheriff or no sheriff."

He spun Partman around, gave him a throw, which sat Partman down in a chair with a crash. Then Canby stepped over to Sax Starke. "When you say you know nothing of Jack Naile's activities, Starke, you lie!"

Sax Starke rocked up on his toes, his face going white. His lips thinned, pulled down at the corners, then he rifled a fist at Reese Canby's face.

Canby avoided the blow only partially, ducking and half turning. Starke's fist glanced off his temple, staggering him, then Starke came in, leaping. And Canby, spinning back at him, smashed Starke in the face, stopping him in his tracks. Starke's chin dropped, and blood trickled over his sagging lip. Before Canby could hit him again, Mason Garr and Bob Stent had pushed between them, with Bob Stent shouldering Canby back.

"Easy, boy—easy!" rapped Stent. "This sort of thing gets nobody nowhere. Starke, you intimated the lie first, so don't get so damned proud when it's thrown back in your *face*."

Mason Garr was restraining Sax Starke, and when Mike Partman would have come out of his chair again, Bert Lanifee snapped, “Stay put, Partman!”

Reese Canby looked across at Sax Starke, bitterly reckless. “One of these days, there’ll be just you and me, Starke. Then we’ll see.”

Sax Starke glared, mopped at his bleeding mouth, and stalked out. Mason Garr turned to Canby, “I’m surprised you brought Naile in alive.”

Canby shrugged, a trifle wearily. “I’m trying to remember there’s such a thing as law. Anything the law can handle, I want to see done that way. I want Naile to face Judge Marland. I’ve been preaching white man’s law to Antone. I’d like to show him an example of it really working. Besides, Naile, dead, couldn’t have talked. Alive, maybc he will. There are things I’d like to know.”

“That,” said Mason Garr, “is fair enough.” The hard-shelled cattleman turned to Mike Partman. “You lock Naile up, you keep him locked up. Savvy?”

Partman nodded sulkily.

They waited until Doc Snell came out. “He’ll live to hang, I hope,” said Doc succinctly. “His kind always do.”

Canby went to see Judge Marland and told his story. Judge Marland nodded quietly. “I appreciate your bringing him in alive, Reese. He’ll stand trial on the charge of attempted murder.”

When Canby went to get his horse, Mason Garr and Bert Lanifee were on the hotel porch talking to Billy Eustace. Canby's horse and Jack Naile's mount had drifted up to the hotel hitch rail of their own accord. Canby started stripping off Naile's saddle and other gear, which he piled on the edge of the porch. He looked at the hotel-keeper.

"Have Pokey Carter lug this gear down to his livery barn, Billy."

"What you going to do with Naile's horse, Reese?" asked Billy.

"Naile killed an Apache bronc. This one goes to the Apaches to replace it."

"An eye for an eye," murmured Billy.

"I can think of worse laws," retorted Canby. He went into the saddle and, with Naile's horse on a lead behind him, rode out of town, taking the Reservation Road.

Billy Eustace looked after him. "If," said Billy gravely, "the cover stays on the pot, there rides the man this whole country can thank for it."

Mason Garr stirred restlessly. "Did I just feel the jab of a needle?"

"I hope so," nodded Billy.

Garr looked down at the Stag Head, where three Tepee horses still stood in front, hip-shot, dozing on three legs in the heat. Garr drew a deep breath.

"Bert, it's about time you and me had a talk with Sax Starke. Come on!"

Watching them, Billy Eustace smiled.

Fox Baraby and Al Sheeve were at the pool table, knocking the balls around. Sax Starke stood at the bar, playing with a whisky glass. Chase Cauley, who ran the Stag Head, a thin, loose-jointed man with a narrow head and face, puttered up and down behind the bar. Starke faced Mason Garr and Bert Lanifee with blank, cold eyes.

It wasn't Mason Garr's way to beat around the bush. His tone was harsh, his words abrupt.

"Sax, you've drifted way off the trail. Get back on it."

Starke understood the challenge. "And if I don't?"

"Why," answered Garr, "Bert and me have decided that you're wrong and Reese Canby is right on this Sentinel Basin deal. So call off your dogs."

Starke repeated his words. "And if I don't?"

"Why," growled Mason Garr, "you'll be traveling all alone. It could turn out—lonesome."

Sax Starke looked them up and down, laughed with open contempt. "That," he jeered, "is what you think." He lifted his glass, emptied it, and moved to the door. "Come on, boys," he called to Sheeve and Baraby.

Antone squatted in the ribboned shade of his jacal and heard Reese Canby through in grave silence, then he spoke slowly.

"This one who would have shot my riders from ambush, why did you not kill him when he was at your mercy, my son?"

"There is the law," answered Canby. "It is not good to strike outside it unless there is no other way. The man will be punished. He will be locked up like some savage animal. The seasons will come and go for many years, and he will still be locked up. This can be even greater punishment than death, Chief."

Antone nodded. "That could be so with some," he agreed. "The horse you brought, it is a good one?"

"Come and see."

Antone rose, followed Reese out into the white sun glare. He walked around the horse that had been Jack Naile's. It was a good horse, a chunky claybank, branded Tepee on the rear foreshoulder. Antone's black eyes brightened.

"It is a good trade," he admitted. "I am content, my son."

Back in the shade of the jacal, Antone ordered a wrinkled crone of a squaw to bring tiswin, the weak Apache beer. Canby drank with him, then rose to leave.

"The other promises I made you have not been forgotten, Antone," Canby said simply. "I ride to make them good."

It was late afternoon before Reese Canby located and got together with Newt Dyas and

Sandy Fossi. They both reported they had seen nothing out of line. When Canby told them of his experience, Sandy exclaimed hotly, "You should have smoked Naile down complete, Reese. Ten to one, he's the same jigger that tried to gulch you out at the home ranch."

"Think so myself," agreed Canby. "But he's better off in jail than dead just now."

Newt Dyas caught Canby's thought. "I dunno, Reese. Tougher stuff in Naile than there was in Rupe Scudder. I doubt he'll talk."

Canby built a smoke. "That you never can tell, Newt. Bars and then a stern judge looking down his throat can do strange things to a man, especially if he gets to thinking that the fellow who put him up to a job is lettin' him drop when the big pinch comes. There's a mean, vindictive streak in Jack Naile. Should he become convinced that he's being let down from higher up, there's no telling which way he'll jump."

Sandy's eyes brightened. "There's another angle. It kind of forces Sax Starke's hand. If he makes a fight for Naile, he's practically admitting that he put Naile up to that job."

Canby grinned. "Keep on thinkin', kid. You'll be a man yet one of these days. How you feelin'?"

"Maybe not quite stout enough to push a mountain down," Sandy shrugged, "but I can still shake along. What do we do now?"

"Things happen, so plans alter. We'll head for town."

Canby, Newt, and Sandy rode into Cassadora through a blue twilight. Canby's first stop was at the jail. Mike Partman was slouched in his office chair, surly and uncommunicative.

"The bird," drawled Canby, "is still in the cage?"

Partman grunted. "There's the key. Take a look for yourself if you don't believe me."

"Why, Mike, you're improving. I wouldn't doubt your word." There was a vast sarcasm in Canby's murmured remark.

Partman glowered at the empty door as Canby left. Mike Partman was a troubled man. The horse he had elected to ride in this whole deal was beginning to show signs of foundering, and he didn't exactly know how to get out of the saddle.

Sandy and Newt had both disappeared when Canby got back on the street. But Canby didn't mind. He knew that Sandy would be at the Stents', while Newt was somewhere around, quiet and dry and self-effacing. Newt would always be somewhere around.

Canby borrowed a razor from Billy Eustace, shaved, had a good wash, and then went into the hotel dining room for supper. Mason Garr, Bert, and Chris Lanifee sat at one of the tables. Garr waved him over.

"Drag up a chair and eat on me," Garr invited.

"You're a kind man, Mason," said Canby, pulling up a chair. "Chris, how long has it been since we ate at the same table? Too long, in my book."

Chris still had that grave look in her eyes, but her manner had mellowed somewhat since the night before. There was even a hint of shyness about her, which made her more girlish and appealing.

Bert Lanifee, always practical, asked, "What did Antone have to say, Reese?"

"Said that the horse was a fair trade. We had a shot of tiswin together. He's still sitting tight."

"That Apache sure puts a lot of trust in you, Reese," said Mason Garr in his blunt way.

Canby shrugged. "His patience surprises me. After all the trust the Apache has shown in the past, only to be double-crossed, a man wonders how they trust anybody at all."

"We had a talk with Sax Starke, Bert and I did," said Garr abruptly.

Something in Garr's tone made Canby lift his head quickly. "What about?"

"We told him we'd come to the conclusion that in the Sentinel Basin deal, you were right and he was wrong. And that if he elected to keep on trying to push things around, he was traveling a lone trail."

Canby's face broke into a wide, welcoming

smile. "As Billy Eustace would say, I feel good—I feel awful good. Bert, Mason—you don't know what this means to me. What it means to Antone and his people. What it means to this whole stretch of country. And it means that all of Starke's bets are coppered now. Yeah, I feel good!"

"About Starke, Reese—don't count him out just yet," said Bert Lanifee gravely. "He made a peculiar crack right after Mason told him off. When Mason told him he'd be traveling a lone trail, Starke laughed and said, 'That's what you think.' "

"He could have been bluffing." Mason Garr growled.

"True. Yet I don't think he was. He's up to something. We'd be fools to take anything for granted. There's a sly depth to Sax Starke that I was too blind to recognize until recently. He'll bear watching," insisted Bert Lanifee.

"We'll watch him," declared Canby, then he laughed softly. "Stopped by the jail when I hit town. By the look of Mike Partman, I'd say he had a bear by the tail and was wondering how he could let go."

"Partman tries to play both ends against the middle." Mason Garr growled. "Damn—excuse me, Chris—darn a man who slips around so you can't put your finger on him. Come next election time, we'll put a man behind that star instead of a worm." The cattleman attacked his steak fiercely.

The meal finished, Mason Garr and Bert Lanifee headed for the Desert House for a game of solo. Reese Canby and Chris Lanifee went out on the hotel porch, pulled up a couple of chairs, and sat there in the soft dark. Pahvant Rim was a towering black presence, the desert a far-running sea of mysterious black. Stars were piling up, shouldering one another about in the velvet heavens. The first coolness of the night was beginning to seep and flow.

Reese Canby was hugely content. The frank admission on the part of Mason Garr and Bert Lanifee that they'd washed their hands of Sax Starke and all his doings was the best kind of news. No longer was he bucking a stiff hand alone. Lacking the support of men like these two, it was hard to see where Starke could do much more than rant and rave. He wouldn't dare.

Canby slouched low in his chair, shoulders hanging loose, the tautness that had been in him so long running out, leaving him fully relaxed. The presence of Chris Lanifee, silent at his side, held him fully quiet and at peace. It was not to last, for Chris spoke suddenly.

"Reese, what about Milt Parrall?"

Canby stirred. "What do you mean, Chris?"

"There's talk that you and he have quarreled, and Milt's been drinking savagely."

"That's true," Canby admitted gravely. "But

I'm telling the truth when I say I haven't the slightest idea what set him off. There's no quarrel on my part, Chris—and I didn't start it. I've been trying to figure an answer, and there just isn't any. No, I don't know what's the matter with Milt."

"I'm afraid I do," said Chris in a small, regretful tone. "And I feel wretched about it."

"I'm listening," said Canby quietly. "You feel wretched—why?"

She took a little time before answering. "I have always liked Mitt, and I knew he liked me. But I had no idea the feeling went deeper with him. I certainly never encouraged him—that much." She hesitated, then took a deep breath and made the plunge. "He asked me to marry him, Reese."

Canby went very, very still. "Yes?"

"I—I tried to get him off the subject. He became insistent. I guess I then went a little short with him. Anyway, he went off, furiously, angry, and then began drinking heavily."

Canby began to stir again.

"Being the kind of person you are, Chris, you'd naturally feel bad about that. Yet it's in no way your fault. In a thing of that sort, a man has to take his chances and, if the nod goes against him, it's one of those things a man has to take and like. I wouldn't worry too much. Milt will probably come around. He'll feel sorry for himself for a while, drink himself into the jitters, and then, some fine day, wake up to the fact he's making the biggest kind of fool of himself. After that, he'll steady down and be the same old Milt again."

"I wonder," murmured Chris. "Sometimes I've wondered if there aren't two Milt Parralls—the one you and I know, and the one we don't know. The thing that makes me feel miserable is the breakup of the friendship between you and Milt. I feel that somehow it's my fault. You see, Reese, he feels that—that if it weren't for you, I'd feel differently about him. There, now I've said it. And I'm glad it's dark so you can't see my face."

Canby got to his feet, caught her hand, and pulled her up to stand beside him.

"Chris, you know how I've always felt about you. It started back when we were kids playing on the reservation together, and it's never changed. Is this the answer I've been waiting for all this time?"

She did not answer immediately, but when Canby gave her a little pull, she swayed toward him. And then her answer came, very soft. "I—I guess it is, Reese."

Reese Canby wondered if it was the thunder of his own pulse that beat across the night, with this girl in his arms and the warm sweetness of her lips against his.

He knew differently the next moment, for all along the street lifted the clamor of voices and the rush of startled and wondering men. Somebody yelled.

"That shot was up at the jail!"

Chris's hands, spread against his chest, pushed him gently away. With rare understanding, she said, "You'll want to go and see, Reese."

Then she was gone, into the hotel. Canby vaulted the porch rail and joined the rush for the jail.

As he ran, he thought he heard the mutter of speeding hoofs, quick fading into the night. By the time he reached Mike Partman's office, the place was crowded. The door to the short hallway leading back to the jail was open. Men were jamming in there, too. Canby used the weight of his shoulders and bulled through the crush.

In the jail, Mike Partman was holding a lamp, looking down at something on the floor under the small barred window of the place. Jack Naile was crumpled there. He was very dead. There was a bullet hole between his eyes, and all around the wound was a blackened area of powder scorch.

To Canby's harsh query, Mike Partman swung his head. There was a dumbfounded, almost stupid look on Partman's face.

"I'm sitting in the door of my office," he mumbled. "I didn't have any light going because I didn't want a flock of bugs winging in. I never heard a sound until the shot. I got this lamp going and tore in here. And there he was, just like you see him."

Partman was telling the truth—Canby could see that. It left only one answer. Jack Naile had no weapon, and if he had had one, he wasn't the sort ever to take his own life. It was plain that he'd been tolled to the window by someone outside and then shot dead in his tracks.

Chapter IX
RENEGADE RENDEZVOUS

Men gathered in Tippo Vance's Desert House to talk things over. Everybody had an idea, but it was Bert Lanifee who voiced the theory running around in Reese Canby's mind.

"Only one reason for it that I can see," said Bert. "Jack Naile knew something that somebody else didn't want known generally. They were afraid Naile might talk, so they took the one sure way to close his mouth."

Mason Garr, still a victim of long habit of thought toward the Apache, grunted. "Maybe, Bert—maybe. On the other hand, it might have been Antone's way of gettin' even—"

"No!" broke in Reese Canby sharply. "You know better than that, Mason. In the first place, Antone doesn't give his word unless he means to keep it. In the second, no Apache could have tolled Naile to that window; Naile was too suspicious a sort for that. The person who got Naile up close to that jail window was somebody he knew and trusted. Bert's given us the logical answer."

"Guess you're right," Garr grumbled crustily. "But what in all-fired hell could he have known that was so important?"

"Maybe," murmured Canby, "the answer as to who the five were who lynched Ponco and Dobe."

"Or," observed Bert Lanifee gravely, "the answer to that crack Sax Starke gave you, Mason, just as he left the Stag Head. About him traveling a lone trail—remember? And he answered, 'That's what you think.' "

Mason Garr shifted uneasily. "When you say that, Bert, you throw a damn serious accusation at Starke. In plain language, you're suggestin' that either at Sax Starke's gun or at his order, Jack Naile got a slug through his head."

Bert Lanifee's lips thinned thoughtfully, then he shrugged. "The way things are breaking in these parts all a man can do is follow logical thought to a logical answer. I'm through trying to make excuses or blind myself to facts. Reese, I don't know what you figure to do next, but here's where I stand. Anything you want of me or my crew, all you have to do is ask. I mean—anything."

"Thanks, Bert. We can't do a thing until we know more. I'll try to find out."

Canby jerked his head to Sandy Foss and Sandy followed him outside. "What now?" asked Sandy.

"Round up Newt Dyas and go back to patrolling Sentinel Basin. The basin is the kernel of this nut."

Newt Dyas's voice, dryly thin and soft, sounded from the shadows. "I scratched some matches and looked for sign outside the jail window, Reese. Some boot prints there, but nothing about them to say for sure whose boots. These blind trails are gettin' on my nerves."

Sandy, who had distinctly jumped when Newt's voice came so unexpectedly from the dark, grumbled.

"Your nerves! How about mine? You scare hell out of me every now and then."

Newt drifted up beside them, a faint thread of humor in his tone. "You look at the stars too much, kid. It's the earth and the things close to it that you got to watch."

They got their horses and left town. Reese Canby looked at the lights of the hotel as they passed, and a great warmth stole through him. Chris was in there. It seemed he could still catch the faint perfume of her hair. And the memory of her lips was a haunting memory to savor and build dreams about . . .

Out at Canby's headquarters, they got a few hours' sleep, but the morning stars were still cold and sharp in an utterly dark sky when they cooked coffee and bacon and breakfasted on these and some cold leftover biscuits.

They talked about Jack Naile and how he had died. Discussion of the why of it always brought them back to the only legitimate answer. Jack

Naile knew something that someone else did not want known. So they had killed him to make sure he never told.

They saddled fresh horses and headed for the north and northwest rim of Sentinel Basin.

"No need guarding farther south," Canby said. "Now that Starke and De Lacca know that Bert Lanifee and Mason Garr are on their toes, there'll be nothing breaking around the black sage country. Any devilment cooked up will come from higher up, where the country is more broken and where it's easier to hide."

"Wish the boys with our herd were down out of the Chevrons," said Sandy. "With them stout rascals to back our hand we could ride right into Tepee, spit in Starke's eye, and tell him to cut his wolf lose."

Canby grinned. "Cows don't move that fast, kid. It'll be a few days yet. You sound like you're gettin' bloodthirsty."

"Not me," denied Sandy. "I'm all for peace an' quiet. But when the thunder begins to roll, I like company."

Canby stationed Sandy virtually at the spot he'd held down the day before, where Jack Naile had appeared. He sent Newt to a spot farther back and lower, from where Newt could keep a long-distance watch on Tepee headquarters.

"I'll be ramming around in the piñon country higher up," Canby explained. "Around noon we'll meet where Sandy is and swap reports on what we see or find—if anything."

It was then dawn and Canby was into the piñons by the time the sun's splendor burst across the world. The air had the vital bite of the night still in it as he sent his horse higher and higher into the piñons. He had no particular destination in mind, no plan beyond a general one of ramming around with his eyes and ears open.

His thoughts switched back and forth, playing for a time on the killing of Jack Naile and on the possibilities which lay behind it. Then, abruptly, he would be back on the porch of Billy Eustace's hotel in the warm, thick dusk, with the wonder of Chris Lanifee's slimness in his arms and the promise of her lips upon his own.

He thought of Milt Parrall and what Chris had said concerning Milt's sudden fit of drinking and astounding change in attitude. At least this offered some explanation for Milt turning on him the way he had. Yet the answer did not fully satisfy. Looking well back, Canby realized that a change had been taking place in Milt Parrall for some time now. It dated back to the day of the trial of Ponco and Dobe. No, it dated even further back, Canby realized soberly, now that he came to think on the matter closely.

Something had begun to build up between him and Milt even before he'd taken his herd up to summer range in the Chevrons. It was something hard to put a finger on, that change in Milt, a gradual creeping up of an invisible walk. Yeah, the old carefree friendship had begun to change months ago. The old heartiness had not come so naturally; it had to be forced.

Canby knew that this change had not come from him. It had started in Milt, who had begun to draw in upon himself. Canby recalled one day when Milt had drifted into such a dark, quiet mood that he'd asked Milt what was troubling him, asked him if he needed money, or something of that sort. And if he needed a loan, all he had to do was ask for it. To both question and offer, Milt had given blunt denial.

Well, mused Canby, if even that far back Milt had figured out what truly lay in Chris Lanifee's mind and heart, he'd been keener in his observations than anybody else had.

Right now, Canby's feeling toward Milt was one of regret and half-formed anger. Regret over a friendship lost and anger that Milt should have taken the attitude he had with Chris Lanifee. To become, as Chris had put it, insistent—so insistent as to make Chris angry. In doing this, Milt had cut himself way down in stature.

A woman's heart was her own, to give as she saw fit. And a man did not bully her if her choice went against him. Something had slipped in Milt. Some deep-hidden and unsuspectedly weak link in the man had snapped. Things, Canby knew, would never be the same again between Milt Parrall and himself, and he felt a bleak regret because of this, for that old friendship had been mighty fine.

The raw bitterness of words and actions Milt had shown that evening in front of the Stag Head Canby was willing to write off as merely whisky talk. Liquor worked that way on some, and many a man had said or done things when inflamed with whisky that he was deeply sorry and remorseful about when soberness returned. Well, Canby mused, he'd told Milt he was leaving the door open, but whether Milt would ever choose to come through it again was anybody's guess.

Midmorning found Canby far up in the piñon hills. He had come up in long, sweeping slants, covering as big a run of country as he could. But he saw nothing beyond an occasional deer and a single late-prowling coyote. This world was big and still, and he had it all to himself.

There was, he finally decided, no point in prowling this country farther. Even if Sax Starke and Chelso De Lacca were cooking up some sort of further nuisance against Sentinel Basin, they'd hardly ride this wide and high a circle. Riding with his thoughts, he had put useless miles behind him.

He broke into a little glade in the piñons and decided that he would turn back from here. And that was when he saw horse sign.

It was fresh, the tracks cutting right through the middle of the glade. They came from below and pointed straight on into the higher, wilder country. Taut with fresh interest, Canby looked them over. A single horse and no stray or half-wild one had made these tracks. And a ridden one, the weight of the rider it carried sinking the hoof marks deeper than if the horse had not been under saddle.

It was possible but not probable for a drifting rider, with no particular goal or purpose, to have ridden this way. A wolf hunter like Henry Joel, maybe. Canby shook his head over this. It wouldn't be Henry Joel, because Joel always had a pack horse tagging behind, carrying his traps and blankets, grub, and other gear. Maybe it was Newt Dyas, who had glimpsed some kind of dcvelopment brewing about Tepee headquarters and was out to find him. That could be it. Canby pointed his horse and followed the sign rapidly.

It led straight upward toward the dim heights of the eastern run of the Chevrons, but within half a mile, swung sharply east. Conviction grew in Canby that this wasn't Newt Dyas he was following. Newt would have cast back and forth across the slope, trying to pick up Canby's trail. This rider moved with a directness that told of definite purpose.

The steady upward drift of tire country broke sharply into comparative level, a wide, long-running benchland, curving east and north. Here the piñons thinned somewhat and, though Canby kept his horse to a rapid walk, caution deepened in him. Nerve ends began to prickle. Whether it was prescience whispering or merely the building tension of pursuit, he could not tell.

A drift of air came across the benchland and touched Canby's nostrils. He set up his horse sharply. The acrid bite of wood smoke rode on the air.

Canby stood high in his stirrups for a long, careful survey of what lay ahead. This was a mistake, for it was from behind him that a voice cut harshly.

"Stay exactly so!"

The click of a gunlock emphasized this order.

Reese Canby did not obey literally. He turned his head. There were two of them, on foot. Both held rifles, both were covering him. Any hostile move on his part would have been swift suicide.

They came up on either side of him, men he had never seen before—shaggy, cold-eyed, and hard-bitten.

"Be real careful while you unbuckle your gun belt and let it drop!" came the order.

With the muzzles of two rifles not four feet from him, there was nothing he could do but obey. Belt and gun thudded to the earth.

"Now you can step down!"

Canby swung out of his saddle. A rifle muzzle jerked.

"That way!"

Canby walked ahead. The two men followed, leading Canby's horse.

A deep anger with himself seethed in Reese Canby. He'd ridden into this thing like some rattle-brained, callow kid. Newt Dyas would never have blundered this way. Newt was too wise. Newt would have followed the sign all right, but he would have made certain what lay along the back trail, too.

The drift of wood smoke grew stronger.

"Turn left!" came the order from behind.

A little ridge, breaking down from higher country and thick furred with piñons, stabbed into the benchland. The ordered way led around the point of it. And here was a camp, with men and horses all about. Nearly a dozen men in all. Canby recognized only one of them. That one was Chelso De Lacca.

A stir of excitement had gone over the camp. A man came up off a pad of blankets where he'd been lounging. He moved with a slight limp. He had bleached ragged hair and a stubble of whiskers about his narrow jaw and tight mouth. His eyes were as blank and restless as a wolf's.

"What is this?" he demanded thinly. "Where'd you get him, Barsey?"

"Back where Roscoe an' me were guardin',"

answered one of Canby's captors. "He was followin' the trail of—him." The speaker jerked his head toward Chelso De Lacca.

The man with the limp turned to De Lacca. "You know him?"

De Lacca's laugh was almost thick with gloating satisfaction. "Know him? Ide, nothing better could have happened. We've picked the joker out of the pack on the first draw. You're lookin' at Mister Reese Canby himself!"

"The hell you say!"

The man with the limp turned for another survey of Canby. "Looks damn ordinary to me," he observed finally. "Well, De Lacca, weren't you just tellin' me that, when an' if we got our hands on him, you wanted him? There he is. Take him!"

Chelso De Lacca laughed again, moistly, savagely gloating. He drew his gun, transferred it to his left hand, and advanced on Canby with his heavy rolling stride. De Lacca wore a dirty bandage under his hat. He stopped a stride from Canby, feet spread, heavy shoulders swaying slightly.

Something cold ran up Reese Canby's spine. Repulsive as Chelso De Lacca had always been to him, with the secretive slyness aswim in his turgid eyes, and the slime of animalism suggested by his manner and looks, he had been almost manly compared to now.

De Lacca's heavy lower lip sagged, his eyes held a reddish glint, and the complete brute was rampant in him. His voice went guttural, thick.

"So—here we are, Canby. And I'm not forgettin' that day in the Desert House. You damned Apache lover!"

De Lacca threw these last words as he threw his right fist. Canby could dodge neither. It was as if a post maul had crashed against the side of his head. He was knocked flat, and he lay there, half-stunned, chaos exploding in his brain. De Lacca moved over and kicked him twice.

"Get up—get up! This is only the start!"

Pain in his head, pain in his body. The sky, the earth, the whole universe a whirling and roaring about him.

Canby got up. He didn't know how or why. Maybe something instinctive in him. Anyhow, he was up, reeling and staggering. He even threw up a warding arm that took part of De Lacca's second blow, so that De Lacca's fist glanced off his head instead of landing squarely.

Reese Canby went down again, but, as was sometimes the case, that second partial blow seemed to unlock the wild numbness the first had brought about. Canby came up fast this time, before De Lacca could kick him again.

Many things limned swiftly on his clearing senses. Every item of this camp seemed to leap out sharply: the fire, with the clutter of smoke-blackened cooking gear about it; the saddles lying here and there; spreads of blankets; unsaddled horses tied among the piñons.

And men. Hard-eyed, hard-faced, watching without the faintest shadow of friendliness or sympathy or pity. Like a circle of wolves they were, calloused, savage, indifferent. Canby knew that nothing to his good would ever come out of them. And here was Chelso De Lacca, one hand holding a gun, the other a pounding, brutal club of a fist. This was bad, very bad. And it would get worse.

It came up out of some depth within him, maybe the depth of utter desperation. Anyway, here it was suddenly—the brightest, coldest anger he had ever known. It ate at him like a flame, urging him to a headlong recklessness, which he fought back doggedly, knowing that if he ever had to use his head, he must use it now. Maybe, by some chance, he could get that gun which De Lacca held . . .

It was a hope soon vanished. Chelso De Lacca, confident that he now had his man where he wanted him, tossed the gun aside and came charging in, both fists balled and swinging.

He ran into the hardest punch Reese Canby had ever thrown in his life. It had fury, desperation, reviving strength behind it. It had all the accumulation of past hatred, aversion, and contempt Canby had always held for Chelso

De Lacca. It laid the left side of De Lacca's face open to the bone.

De Lacca grunted like an axed hog, but he did not go down. The blow did stop his rush, stopped it cold. He stood there, wavering slightly, feet spread, knees rubbery. Canby's arm was numb to the shoulder from the force of the punch.

A cry broke from Chelso De Lacca's lips. It was like the blubbery bawl of some animal out of a dark pit, then he came lunging in again.

Reese hit him twice more, right and left, but the blows had no discernible effect. He did not get away fast enough. De Lacca, clawing and mauling now, caught hold of him, jerked him close, wrapped both arms around him in the hug of a maddened bear. Canby had just time to slide both hands up before the stricture set down. He jabbed them under De Lacca's sagging, blood-spattered chin and locked his fingers in De Lacca's thick throat.

Canby wondered how much a man's spine could stand before it broke. He had never known agony even remotely comparable to that which racked him now. He could feel his ribs spring, and he thought they must crumple, too. Yet, all this sheer torture added strength to his own fingers. It was an outlet for pain. His fingers dug deeper and deeper, past the set muscles in De Lacca's gross throat, biting for the life.

De Lacca's mouth opened wide. His need and

hunger for air set up a frantic gasping, a harsh wheezing. His eyes began to bulge, his tongue protrude. The terrible pressure of his arms lessened, then fell away entirely, and he began clawing madly at Canby's wrists, trying to tear that strangling grip away.

Canby hung on, blindly desperate, sobbing air back into his tortured lungs. He braced himself, hunched a knee, and drove it into De Lacca's body again and again. De Lacca gave back, shambling heavily, the brute power running out of him. He fell, dragging Reese Canby down on top of him. The left side of De Lacca's face was all wet crimson, the right turning dark with congestion. There had been few rules when this began, there were none at all now. This was only the law of the jungle, elemental, brutal—kill or be killed.

Chelso De Lacca was like some monster in its death agonies. Over and over he rolled, legs kicking, arms flailing in blind madness. Anything to shake loose that grip on his throat. He couldn't do it. He could not tear away from Reese Canby's locked fingers.

De Lacca's wild tumbling ceased. He began to shudder. His face was purple now, his eyes protruding in a wild, glazed glare. His back arched in one final dreadful effort, then he sagged down, ponderously limp and flaccid.

That was when Ide, leader of this wild crowd,

stepped up, and slapped Reese Canby across the head with the barrel of a six-shooter. Canby slumped like a dead man.

Hours had passed; it was twilight. Consciousness had come back to Reese Canby some time before, but he gave no sign of it. He lay still, eyes closed, waiting out the rioting torture in his clubbed head. He tried to think, but it seemed that nothing would stay long enough in his brain to become fully coherent. The physical, it seemed, had to come back before the mental would function properly.

There were voices about him, but at first, they seemed far away and vaguely disembodied, like echoes coming out of some distant darkness. Gradually, the drone of them cut deeper and deeper into his reviving senses. Then, without warning, someone sloshed a hatful of icy water on his face and head. This thoroughly shook him out of the hazy half-world he'd been drifting through. He opened his eyes, blinking painfully until some measure of proportion and orientation returned. He found himself looking up at Saxon Starke.

There was a strange look on Sax Starke's face. Mainly, it was a look of cold hate, but in it was also something of superstition, almost of fear. Someone was speaking.

"You can believe it or not, Starke, but I'm

tellin' you again, he beat De Lacca with his bare hands, beat him after De Lacca had first punch. And he'd have killed De Lacca with those same bare hands if I hadn't gun-whipped him. This here is a tough fightin' man, Starke. I've never seen a better one."

"Well," said Starke harshly, "there's no fight left in him now. Why isn't he tied up?"

"Hardly necessary, do you think? After all, me and my boys ain't school kids."

"What do you intend doing with him, Ide?"

"Mebbe you better answer that question. De Lacca said he wanted him. I told De Lacca to take him. You see the shape De Lacca's in. What's your idea?"

What Sax Starke wanted to do showed in the look in his eyes and the fact that he half-drew his gun. Reese Canby swallowed thickly and spoke with a harsh painfulness.

"That wouldn't settle things as simply as you think, Starke. You've already cut a lot of strings behind you. Gunning me would be the final one. This country would kill you or run you to death. You see, there's been a big shift of opinion by a lot of important people."

Sax Starke's lips peeled back. "They'd never know where or how you died, Canby."

"So you say," Canby retorted. "You've always made one big mistake. You figure everybody is a fool but yourself. These hills have more eyes and ears than you dream of. Alive, I could be of some worth in a trade. Dead, I'd be worth nothing except to my friends. I got quite a few of them. Better think it over, Starke."

Starke cursed, drew his gun fully. "I don't know what I'm waiting for—!" He pushed the muzzle of the gun at Canby.

"I do!" It was Ide, leader of the wild crew. He shoved Starke's gun out of line. "Suppose we wait a bit, Starke. This fellow just gave me a thought. He mentioned a trade. Now that makes sense. That's what me and my boys are sittin' into this game for—a trade. We ain't up here for our health. Starke, put your gun away!"

Starke swung his head angrily. "Damn it, Ide, keep out of this! I brought you up here to—"

"You didn't bring me up here to go high and mighty on me, Starke," cut in Ide coldly. "Don't try it on me. Let's get one thing clear and straight right here and now. Strictly man to man, you don't mean a damn thing more to me than does this fellow Canby. Everything is strictly business with me and my boys. Show us where we can make a profit, and we string along. That's all we're interested in—money in our jeans. There's a point in what Canby said. Dead, he's a total loss. Alive, he could be profit. So, he lives while I think on it."

"I've already explained where the profit is for

you," argued Sax Starke. "I've promised you cattle—"

"Sure. Apache cattle, when and if we get 'em. That 'if' could be a big one. But Canby—why, he's right here at my feet. There's no 'if' there."

"But I've given you my promise," stormed Starke again. "And when I make a promise—"

Ide cut him short with a hard gesture. "Let's have no more talk about promises. I don't believe in 'em. Just now I saw you ready to gun a man lyin' helpless at your feet. Me, I'm no angel. I've smoked down my share of men, and I'll probably smoke down more before I'm done. But I never shot a man flat on his back when he had no single chance for his alley. But you were ready to. And then you got the nerve to ask me to believe your promise. In some things, Starke, you and me are alike. In some things, we're different. We're both crooks. I admit it and don't give a damn. But you'd pose as an honest man. Your promise—" Ide snapped his fingers derisively. Sax Starke was dark with wild, banked fury, but he knew better than to let it get the better of him. He choked it back and said almost steadily, "Then you don't intend to go along?"

"Of course I intend to go along," rapped Ide. "Why do you think I'm here, if not to go along? We've a deal cooked up, you and me. With luck, we both profit; it's strict business all the way. But for God's sake, that don't mean I got to like you or trust you any further than I can jump. As for Canby, well, if things turn out good, maybe I'll make you a present of him, to do with as you damn please. But for the present, I keep him, maybe as a sort of guarantee. Yeah, a guarantee. See what I mean, Starke?" A thin, cold smile was on Ide's lips as he finished.

He did not wait for Starke to reply but turned to one of his men. "Tie Canby up, Duke."

"I could stand a drink of water," said Reese Canby.

"Sure," Ide nodded. "Give him a drink first, Duke."

The drink helped a lot. And it wasn't too bad after that, even though his wrists and ankles were bound. At least he was alive, and he was able to squirm around until he found a reasonably comfortable position. His head ached savagely, but the clubbed numbness was leaving it. His thoughts were clear, no longer fumbling. His back and chest muscles had stiffened up from the mauling they had taken under the pressure of Chelso De Lacca's bear hug, and the side of his head, where De Lacca's first and only good blow had landed, was bruised and sore. But in the main, Reese Canby was feeling much better.

The wild crew had a fire going, were cooking coffee and bacon. The savory odors set the juices in Canby's mouth working. When Ide, moving about with a certain wild restlessness which seemed a definite part of the man, limped past, Canby spoke quietly.

"I'll be just as dead if I'm starved to death as I would if Starke had shot me."

Ide did not answer, but after those about the fire had eaten, the fellow called Duke brought a cup of coffee and a measure of food over, untied Canby's hands, boosted him to a sitting position, then squatted silently by while Canby ate and drank.

Canby's shirt was torn and spattered with the blood of Chelso De Lacca, but in the breast pocket of it was still a limp sack of tobacco and some papers. Canby flexed his stiffened fingers and fumbled a cigarette into shape. Duke, lighting a smoke of his own, held the match to Canby's cigarette. Canby inhaled deeply and murmured, "Thanks."

Duke tied him up again and went back to the fire.

Canby lay quiet, thinking. It had been a terrific day. Here, he mused, lay the answer to Sax Starke's remark that had kept Bert Lanifee wondering. This fellow Ide and his men were Starke's ace in the hole. It was plain that Starke had realized some time ago that he could not count on the continued backing of such men as Bert Lanifee and Mason Garr. That support had begun to slip away from him when the cattle-rustling charge against Ponco and Dobe had turned out to be such a fraud. The subsequent lynching of the two Apache riders had further alienated such support. Nor had it succeeded in making Antone and his people jump the barrier that would bring about the governmental interference which Starke was gambling for.

So, Sax Starke and Chelso De Lacca had gone farther afield. They had brought in Ide and his men for some kind of rustling deal against the Apache herds, knowing that here indeed would the Apache fight. That was what Starke wanted. He wanted Antone and his men to make this thing a shooting war. Once that came about, the door to Sentinel Basin would be unlocked.

While waiting for this to develop, Starke had tried another angle. He had turned Jack Naile loose on a dry-gulching trail. Further persecution of the Apache. Anything to cause a break. But that had failed, too. And now Jack Naile was dead. Here, figured Reese Canby, was the answer to Naile's death. Naile knew that Starke and De Lacca were bringing in Ide and the wild crowd. If that knowledge got past his lips before Starke and Ide were ready to strike at the Apache herd, then there would be all hell to pay. So Starke had made certain Naile would never tell.

Canby smiled bleakly in the darkness. No wonder Starke wanted to gun him while he lay helpless. There had always been that antagonism between them. And then he had blocked every move of Starke's so far. He'd shown up Starke's hand in the rustling trial. He'd kept Antone and his braves from striking back after the lynching. He had ended Jack Naile's dry-gulching trail and again kept Antone quiet. Yeah. Starke had plenty of cause to hate him and wish him dead.

This fellow Ide and his men—all were strangers to Canby. That they were outlaw breed, there was no question. Ide had stated as much, callously enough, knowing Canby heard every word and not caring. A rough, tough, ruthless crew, these. Probably from the canyon and basin country over past the Chevrons. That was wild, lonely country where the law didn't reach. It held many like Ide and his gang.

Canby had no illusions concerning this outlaw, Ide. He knew he had heard the truth when Ide told Starke that only one thing had brought him and his men into these parts. Profit—money, or the promise of it in their jeans. Apache cattle, the bait was. A strong, surprise raid and a herd of Apache cattle choused out of Sentinel Basin and driven deep into the outlaw wilderness, and somewhere back there, turned into the profit Ide spoke of.

The deal probably would be that Tepee would help Ide's crowd in the steal but ask for none of the rustled cattle as their share. All they wanted was for Antone to start shooting and so forfeit all sympathy with the powers that were.

These were the answers Reese's thoughts brought to him. They were the general answers. But how about the personal one? How about him? He didn't try to delude himself. While Ide figured he might be of some value, he would live. Once Ide decided the value was not there, death would be certain.

But what would this value be, and how would Ide be calculating it? Maybe as a club to hold over Starke and De Lacca, a threat to force a fatter deal out of the Tepee owners. Canby smiled again, sardonically now. It was the old story of no honor among thieves. Neither honor nor trust nor conscience.

Now that his strength was back, Canby began working quietly at his bonds. He soon gave up. No hope here. Duke had put those bonds on to stay. So a man could only be fatalistic about this thing. While he lived, some hope was obtained. While he lived . . . !

Sax Starke and Ide had settled by the fire and were talking back and forth. Over some points, they argued; on others, they agreed. Their voices were low, and Canby could not get what they were saying. Only their gestures told anything. Apparently, Ide was driving a stiffer bargain than Starke had figured on. It was plain that Starke was still angry. Even the flickering, tricky light of the fire could not disguise the hard twist of his lips. Finally, Canby saw him nod, then nod again.

Starke stood up, looked over to where Canby lay, and in that look was a bleak and savage promise. Starke moved back to the faint edge of the firelight, leaned over, and said something to someone on the ground. A hulking figure crawled unsteadily erect. Chelso De Lacca. Starke had to steady him as they moved away into the blackness. Presently, the muffled clump of departing hoofs sounded, soon to fade out completely.

Ide got up, made his restless, limping prowl about the fire. He came over to Canby and stood staring down at him. It was too dark for Canby to make out the outlaw's expression. Ide called abruptly, "You sure you got this fellow Canby tied plenty tight, Duke? He's worth money to us now."

"He'll keep, Harry," answered Duke. "Starke wants him five thousand dollars' worth, eh?"

"That's right. I had to really twist Starke's tail to get it. But I had him over a barrel, and he knew it. While Canby lives, he blocks the trail to Sentinel Basin. Alive and loose, knowing what he knows now, he'd be a sure noose around Starke's neck. Once he spread the word, he'd have every man in this part of the state gunning for Starke. And there'd go Starke's great dream of Sentinel Basin grass."

"Maybe they'll go gunning for Starke anyhow, when Canby turns up missing," said another of the group.

"That's the gamble Starke has to take. It's not too long a one. Canby disappears, nobody knows how, nobody knows where. Nobody can really prove a thing. So Starke could ride that out, all right. Well, it's nothin' to us either way as long as we get our cut. Duke, you and Barsey take turns guardin' for the night. The rest of us will get some sleep. Tomorrow could be quite a day."

Duke brought a saddle and blanket over by Reese Canby. He propped himself up against the saddle, wrapped himself in the blanket, and settled back, the smoke of his cigarette tangy in the dark. The rest of the crew rolled up closer to the fire, which had begun to flicker low. There was a scattering of murmured remarks, then these ran out and quiet settled in. The fire went to nothing but coals, which made a faint dry crackling as they one by one dissolved into ash.

The darkness thickened and grew cold. At the far edge of the camp, where the piñons massed blackly, a tired horse stamped once and sighed deeply. Silence held the world.

The cold bit deep into Reese Canby. A blanket would have helped mightily, but no one gave a damn about that, apparently. So Canby set himself to endure the discomfort of the night. He even fell asleep.

Midnight stars were frigid in the sky when he awoke. There was a stir beside him, the low mutter of voices. It was Barsey, taking over the guard from Duke. Reese Canby thought he was frozen. This camp was high in the piñon hills, and the night was cruel. He had to clench his teeth to keep them from chattering. Shivers ran through him.

"How's for a blanket?" he mumbled.

"Hell with you," answered Barsey callously. "Shut up!"

Canby tried to go back to sleep again, but without success. Physical misery was too dominant. His arms and wrists and hands seemed dead from the stricture of the bonds, from the cold. There was no comfort in the earth now. It, too, was cold and hard and unyielding. From now until dawn was going to be a long, long wait.

To get his mind off his misery, Canby tried to lure other thoughts, any kind of thoughts. None of them stayed long with him. A queer feeling came over him. It was as though time was thrown all out of balance. Yesterday, the day before—incredibly far away. Even this morning, or maybe it was yesterday morning by this time, when he'd watched the dawn come up, when he'd been his own man, riding free and strong and confident through the piñons—that also seemed something out of the distant past. He didn't think of the future, because as things stood now, there wasn't any. He was some infinitesimal atom of matter, floating around in space, half alive, half dead, and of no consequence at all . . .

Time pulled another funny one on him. Maybe he'd gone out, with outraged nature having her say. Anyhow, he had the feeling that more hours had passed, though the black was still Stygian here among the piñons, here on this lofty heave of the world. For one crazy moment, he felt that he was all alone in a lost world, then he knew better.

Beside him sounded a stir, a faint slithering thud. Then a long, failing sigh, like breath running out of something, never to come back. While Canby was trying to puzzle this out, a hand found his lips and settled there. And then a man's head, pressing close to his, and words in his ear in a whisper faint as a star fall.

"This is Newt. I had to knife the guard. There was no other way. Quiet!"

Chapter X
DEATH AT DAWN

The slow ebb of Reese Canby's pulse became a surging tide. Newt Dyas's presence and whispered words had the impact of some powerful stimulant. The settled chill of the hours was miraculously gone from Canby's numbed and stiffened body. Abruptly, he was warm all through, his senses sharp and biting.

He felt Newt's knife slip down between his bound wrists, and presently, his hands were free. Then his ankles. He felt Newt working at his spurs, which were noiselessly removed and put aside. Then Newt's thin, soft whisper in his ear again. "I'll drag you. Give me what help you can. But—quiet!"

Newt had him by the shoulder, with a strong, slow pull. They gained a little ground. Canby was of little help. His hands and feet were like useless clubs. Within his body, life surged hot and eager, but that returning energy had not yet reached the extremities. And the muscles of his back were like creaking boards, and the stirring pain in them was an edged knife. So, for a little way, Newt had to do it all.

It was desperately slow business. Canby marveled that Newt found purchase to move him at all. Then he found that by lying flat on his back, he could dig in his elbows and give a slight lift when Newt pulled. This gained ground faster, but at best, it was snail-pace movement. And the tension of the moment rasped across a man's nerve ends until they were raw and quivering.

Another torment came to Canby. Returning circulation reached his hands and feet and brought with it an agony so exquisite, he had to grit his teeth from crying aloud. Yet it was a price he was glad to pay, for slowly his hands and feet began to obey the press of his will. He not only dug in his elbows but his heels as well, and this added purchase gained precious distance by the foot where inches measured it before.

He spread his hands flat on the earth, gripped it with spread fingers, forcing them to work, driving the numbed clumsiness out of them. Moisture trickled down his bitterly set jaw, and he was amazed to realize that now, despite the frigid night, he was sweating.

Came Newt's whisper again, exultant now, "Rest a minute. We're doin' fine!"

Reese Canby listened for a moment, in a night that seemed poised and breathless. It was good to be sweating, for the sweat was an oil to numbed and stiffened muscles. His whole physical being began to respond more and more as they edged farther from the confines of the camp.

Newt murmured, “Roll over and crawl. Hang on to my foot!”

That was the way it was, and now they were creeping into the close-packed boles of piñon trees. They were at the lower reach of that heavily timbered ridge that thrust out into the benchland by the outlaw camp.

At the far side of the camp, a horse stamped restlessly. A blanketed figure by the dead coals of the fire rose to one elbow. The voice of Harry Ide, the outlaw leader, cut through the dark, “Everything all right, Barsey?”

There was no answer, and Ide came fully out of his blanket and limped across to where prisoner and guard had been. A moment later, his yell smashed across the night.

“Everybody up—everybody up! Barsey’s dead, and Canby’s gone. Up and out—everybody!”

There was the inevitable moment of blind, fumbling confusion. Men were lunging and cursing about in the dark, driving their sleep-drugged wits to some measure of coherency. Newt Dyas seized on this moment.

“Up and travel!” he hissed. “We’ve had our break.”

He pushed a six-shooter into Canby’s hand. Then they were on their feet, breasting the rise of the ridge.

Harry Ide had either the ears or the eyes or the instinct of some night animal, or perhaps a measure of all three. At any rate, gun flame split the dark, and the bellow of report sent cold echoes rumbling. The bullet thudded into a piñon not a yard from Canby's head.

"The ridge!" yelled Ide. "Comb that ridge!"

Newt and Canby went up the ridge slope at a blind, scrambling run. At first, there was a maddening clumsiness in Canby's legs and feet, and this, combined with the steepness of the ridge slope and the thick growth of piñons, held him back. Newt Dyas, a lank ghost of a man, with all the sharpened senses that a lifetime of wilderness prowling had given him, could have been gone in a moment, but he stayed with Canby, helping him, guiding him.

"Go on, Newt—go on!" gulped Canby. "You've done more than enough for me. Get out of here! I'll take my—"

"Shut up!" snapped Newt. "Save your breath."

They fought on up the ridge. Behind them, they could hear Harry Ide's shouting. Some of his men he was sending up the ridge afoot, others he had catching and saddling. Gunfire bombed the night again and again, lead whipping and snapping among the piñons of the ridge.

Canby and Newt made no attempt to shoot back. Driving effort brought back physical balance to Canby in an ever-surging tide. His feet were not so clumsy, his balance better. By the feel of the lessening slope under them, they knew they had gained the crest of the ridge. They turned along this, still climbing, but with less effort now. They could see better now, the glint of the stars lancing straight down, showing some small interval here and there among the close-packed piñons. They moved faster.

They heard pounding hoofs racing below them, whipping along the base of the ridge on either side, driving up to pinch off escape higher along the ridge. And men on foot were combing the ridge proper, crashing and fumbling, cursing in the dark.

Breath surged in and out of Canby's lungs in a hard panting. The violent effort of the climb set up pounding in Canby's head to awaken full pain again. But he plunged on, following the vague, flitting thing that was Newt Dyas.

Here, the ridge humped up sharply, then fell to an equally sharp slope, breaking down into a little dark pocket thickly massed with growth.

Newt said, "Wait here!"

Canby caught at a handy tree trunk, dropped his head on his arm, and sucked greedily for air. The beating pain in his clubbed head was the worst. If that would only lessen, he thought, he'd have felt reasonably normal. Even so, the short rest did him good.

Newt came back to him, leading a horse. The animal was restless, snorting softly.

"Get aboard, Reese," ordered Newt in a thin,

dry murmur. "I'll lead the bronc until we get out of this tangle, then we'll make a run for it. The bronc can carry double."

Canby did not argue. Newt knew what he was doing. Good old Newt. Given half a chance, Newt would make monkeys out of Harry Ide and his renegade gang. In the old days, as a civilian scout and guide for Crook, Newt had fooled even the Apaches. And when you could do that, you were good.

Canby crouched low in the saddle, hands locked on the saddle horn, his head dropped against the cushion of his forearms. He felt brush and low-hung branches whip against his legs and slide over the bowed round of his shoulders. The way pitched downward, the horse moving with bunched haunches and sharp-placed forefeet.

Canby could hear the renegade gang calling back and forth; once or twice, a gun snarled as some pursuer thought he had the quarry located. No lead came near. There was a crashing higher up now, where riders were slicing across the ridge, blocking that way out. But Newt wasn't trying to follow the backbone of the ridge. He was cutting down the side of it now, to the southwest, aiming to break clear through the interval between the renegades on foot and those in the saddle.

The horse stopped. Canby lifted his head. His breath was running more easily now, the pounding in his head lessened somewhat. He was surprised to find the world gray about him. Dawn was breaking. Newt had disappeared, but in a moment he was back. He swung up behind Canby, reached past him and took the reins.

"Hang on," he murmured. "This is it!"

They were completely clear of the ridge and its black tangle. Newt held the horse to a walk. The dawn light was spreading, the stars paled and gone. After the massed growth on the ridge, this wide benchland seemed park-like with its meadows and openings.

They gained a good hundred yards before a wild yell lifted from the base of the ridge. A gun blared, and a slug whipped by. Newt gigged the horse into a run, and the pound of hoofs echoed behind them. After that, it became a race.

Renegade riders stormed down off the ridge; those on foot went plunging back to get their mounts. The lightening vistas of the benchland seemed full of flitting figures. But Newt Dyas's cunning had won him and Canby a break. Now it was up to the horse under them.

The chill morning air beat against Canby's face, whistled past his ears. The bite of it cleared his head, and he rode fully erect, instinctively beginning to judge the pace of this horse and how much strength it had to keep going, carrying a double burden. Surely not enough to carry them down out of the hills and to the safety of the lower country.

Ide and his renegade crew could be counted upon to do their damnedest to kill or capture him again. He knew too much now. He knew enough, if he could make his escape good, to smash Sax Starke and all his scheming completely. He knew enough to break up any rustling ideas on the part of Ide and his men. And he represented five thousand dollars fleeing away from them, the five thousand Sax Starke was willing to pay to get his hands on him again, with no one to call off Starke's gun.

The mathematics of the thing were all against him and Newt. This horse couldn't outrun those coming up behind, not while it carried two riders. Even now, while the horse was fairly fresh, it was losing ground to the pursuit. Guns began to rip and snarl from behind, and lead whistled and whipped by.

Newt seemed to understand Canby's thoughts. With his chin hard set on Canby's shoulder, Newt said, "With luck, there's a surprise waiting for this gang. I think this bronc's got enough to get us there."

They hit the edge of the benchland, and before them, in the growing day, lay the far, sloping downbreak of the main mountain flank and the deep gulf, still in shadow, of the black sage range, of Sentinel Basin, of the desert, and all the world beyond.

The horse was beginning to labor now. It had made a gallant run, but it was just about through. Newt took the slope at an angle to the west and now sent a long yell reaching out ahead.

"Sandy! Sandy Foss!"

To Canby's amazement, an answer came back from below. And now Canby glimpsed, breaking up the slope to meet them at a driving run, a dark mass of riders.

Newt said, "Friends, Reese."

Right after that, Canby heard the bullet hit. He thought it was the horse, and he said, "Pull up, Newt—pull up! The bronc will be going out from under us—!"

Newt didn't answer. Pitched forward by the slope, he lay heavily against Canby's back. His hands holding the reins dropped lower and lower, fell away completely. Canby grabbed the reins just before they slipped from Newt's fingers. And now Canby understood. It was Newt that had been hit.

He swung an arm behind him, trying to hold Newt up, while at the same time bringing the plunging horse to a halt. The animal brought up, swinging its haunches downslope. Newt tipped and slid, getting away from Canby's frantic grab, hitting the ground and rolling, to bring up against a piñon twenty feet down.

Canby went out of the saddle, slid down beside Newt, who lay in a limp heap. Canby caught at him.

"Newt! Newt, old man—!"

He got Newt partially straightened out. Then Canby crouched there, oblivious to everything, deep sunk in the coldest bitterness and grief a man could know. Newt Dyas was dead. He'd been dead within a heartbeat after that bullet hit, the bullet that would have surely killed him, Reese Canby, if Newt hadn't been riding behind him to take the slug . . .

Riders stormed past, racing upslope. Guns were crashing all about him. Men were shouting. The deep, harsh roar of Mason Garr, a gray, wicked old wolf, at a time like this. And Sandy Foss calling, "Reese! You all right, Reese?"

Then a horse, plunging to a halt close beside. And Sandy, dropping on one knee, grabbing him by the shoulder, shaking him.

"Reese! You're not hit?"

Canby lifted a haggard, bitter face.

"Newt! He's gone, kid. They killed Newt!"

Sandy swore bleakly, but was practical against the urge of the moment.

"We got a fight on our hands, Reese, and need every gun."

Canby lingered to drop a hand on Newt's still shoulder, then he was driving upslope to Newt's horse. He didn't know how it had happened that

Sandy was here, and Mason Garr and others, but they were, and they were moving up to meet Harry Ide and his crowd head-on. For himself, Canby wanted Ide. He wanted any of that gang he could get. He wanted all of them—to pay for Newt.

He swung the horse below him and went into the saddle. Newt's rifle was in its boot, under the stirrup leather. He dragged it out and sent the horse back up the slope. Sandy and Mason Garr and the others were already well above him, guns throwing an uneven tolling across the slope. The renegade gang, running into something they had not expected, had broken and scattered somewhat. But they were beginning to organize up there.

The horse, blown though it was, did pretty well with only one man up. Reese Canby moved by instinct alone, for his mind was still too locked by tragedy to work with conscious logic. Yet the thing he did instinctively was the right thing. He did not follow Sandy and Mason Garr and the others straight up. Instead, he swung around the slope to the west and then began the climb. He broke over the crest into the comparative level of the benchland, headed in on the flank of the renegades. Their attention was down, where Sandy and Mason Garr were moving in. Canby saw Harry Ide standing high in his stirrups, placing his men along the advantage of the crest.

Canby stopped his horse, swung from the saddle, and dropped to one knee. He looked down the sights of Newt Dyas's rifle. He saw the figure of Ide through them, and he pressed the trigger. Past the recoil of the rifle he saw Ide lunge far forward and roll out of his saddle. Canby swung the lever of his weapon, started to get to his feet, sank back to his knee again as another renegade ran over to Ide, bent over him, straightened, and looked wildly around. Canby's second bullet took the fellow fair. He jackknifed down beside his dead leader.

Canby got to his feet and walked steadily forward. He was a cold, emotionless killing machine. Through his mind two words ran, over and over, like the tolling of some great bell, "For Newt—for Newt!"

He shot twice more. He killed a renegade's horse with one shot and knocked the renegade kicking with the second. This flank attack broke the solidarity of the renegades. Their leader and two more of their number down. Gunfire from in front and from the flank. They broke and rode for it. Some of them fired at Canby, and their lead spattered and thudded all about him. He felt the wind of one bullet against his face; another tugged at a loose fold of his tattered shirt. He gave them no drought at all, just trying to find another target for this deadly rifle of Newt's.

But the targets were swift-flitting and gone, and

now it was Sandy and Mason Garr and the men with them bursting over the crest and racing out across the bench-land after the fleeing renegades.

A strange tightness had formed at the base of Canby's skull. It spread all through his head, seeming to squeeze his brain to nothingness. He stumbled and weaved. The world began to whirl crazily. A far-off, hardly felt blow struck him. He did not know it was the impact of the ground as he fell. He drifted far down into dark, dizzy depths . . .

The raw bite of whisky burned all through him, set him to a strangled coughing. The world and all that was in it came back to him. He was lying on his back, a folded jumper under his head. His head was wet, and somebody was working at it. Sandy Foss was, with Mason Garr, crouched beside him. Their eyes were anxious.

"Where'd I get hit?" he mumbled dully.

"You didn't," answered Sandy. "Mason an' me, we can't find no bullet hole, but by and large, you look like you'd been run over by a freight train. Good Lord, Reese, what did they do to you?"

Canby shrugged. "Enough. How'd it happen you fellows showed up just in time?"

He lay quiet while Sandy told the story. How Newt Dyas, keeping watch over the Tepee headquarters, had seen a strange rider breaking down out of the high piñon country and drifting in to

Tepee. A little later, accompanied by Sax Starke, this rider had headed back to the high country again. Newt had trailed them all the way to the renegade camp. Newt had seen Canby there, a prisoner. He had ridden out again, found Sandy, and told him what had happened. Sandy was to head back to Cassadora, gather up what help he could find, and come back to the piñon country along a certain way.

Newt was to Injun up on the renegade camp again, break Canby free if he could. If there was no chance of this, then he would turn back, meet Sandy and the others, and lead them to a surprise attack on the renegade outfit.

Well, Newt had broken Canby loose, and now Newt was dead.

Canby felt better when they got him into the saddle again. That last spasm in his beaten head seemed to have been something that had to come and go again before his head would straighten out. Now he felt beaten and weary and old, riding through a gray and brutal world, as they went back to where Newt Dyas lay.

These men Sandy had brought were made up of Mason Garr's and Bert Lanifee's crews. Bert Lanifee had wanted to come along the worst way, so Mason Garr said, but that bad leg of his was too much of a handicap to take into the hills on a saddle. And the renegade crew were thoroughly broken and scattered, Garr added.

"You raised hell with them when you hit 'em from the flank, Reese," said Garr bluntly. "But for that, it could have worked into a wicked showdown. We wouldn't all be riding out of this with whole skins."

All but Newt.

They rode down out of the hills and into Bert Lanifee's Trumpet headquarters. They carried Newt across his own saddle. Canby rode the horse of a dead renegade.

Bert Lanifee was at Trumpet, but Chris, so Bert explained, was still in town. He had made her stay there, what with things breaking so wild. It was safer.

Reese Canby drank black coffee and ate food that he did not taste. He told his whole story to a circle of grim, silent men. He told of the words he'd heard pass between Sax Starke and Harry Ide. He told of his fight with Chelso De Lacca. He told of Sax Starke standing over him when he was down and helpless, ready to gun him, and of Starke's rage at being held back by Harry Ide, so the outlaw could bargain for Canby's life, as he might for a beef critter up for slaughter.

Mason Garr cursed harshly. "Starke and De Lacca—they've gone raving crazy. That must have—!"

"No," cut in Canby. "They're no different than they ever were, Mason. It's just that events are uncovering what's always been inside them."

“We will run them out of this country,” vowed Bert Lanifee. “They’re a menace to every decent person in it. We’ll ride right now and—”

Canby shook his head. “My chore, Bert. I took it on. I’ll finish it.” His lips thinned, pulled down at the corners. “I’m gettin’ more reasons all the time. You fellows were great, coming through like you did on this last deal. I can’t have anybody else going out on my account, like Newt Dyas did. This thing will finish one of these days, and if I’m still alive, I don’t want any more like Newt on my conscience. Hold tight. Right now, Starke and De Lacca stand blocked again. Their rustling deal has gone up in smoke.”

They buried Newt Dyas on a little flat, back under the massive sweep of Pahvant Rim. No man would ever have a more eternal headstone. Come what would, Pahvant Rim would stand, smoldering and blazing under sunlight, dark and rugged under storm. Only the final cataclysm of all earthly things, the breakup of the universe itself, could change the rim. And at that time, it wouldn’t matter, anyhow.

Reese Canby had a scalding hot bath and donned clean clothes, which Bert Lanifee supplied, then he sprawled on a bunk, sought sleep, found it finally, and was like a dead man for the rest of the day. He awoke in a cooling world, with blue dusk closing down. He got up and worked the stiffness out of his back and shoulders, where the bruises from Chelso De Lacca's ponderous fists and arms still lay dark and angry.

He sent Sandy Foss back to town. "Just stay put, kid. Keep your eyes and ears open. Don't get too far from Mary Stent."

Sandy's eyes went cold. "De Lacca shows around, I'll blow his head off."

"If he does, you do it, kid. And aim straight. That's what things have come to."

"Where you going?"

"Out to see Antone. I'll see you in town later."

It was a soft land at night. The earth sent up the day's heat and called in the cooling breath of the stars. The smell of space and the eternal hills was there, good in a man's lungs. Canby twisted once in his saddle, looked back to where Pahvant Rim laid a black limit to the downward curve of the velvet, star-spangled heavens. Newt was over there, at his last long rest. He wouldn't be forgotten. It took a good man to leave behind the kind of memories Newt had left . . .

There was a definite tension in the Apache rancheria. Canby had to pass the usual guards. Antone came out from the gloom of his jacal to greet Canby, something unusual in itself.

"I am glad you have come, my son," said the old chief. "I have broken my given word. You see me in my shame. I will go with you, and the white man's law can have its way with me."

Canby, startled, said, "I do not understand."

"Come," said Antone quietly.

He led the way to a small jacal where complete silence held. Faint starlight filtered through. Canby glimpsed the outline of two prone figures, like sleeping men.

"Look, and you will understand," said Antone.

Canby scratched a match, cupped the faint flare, and had his look. The dead faces of Fox Baraby and Al Sheeve looked back at him. The match went out.

Canby said, "Tell me."

There wasn't much. Apache riders had come across Baraby and Sheeve deep in Sentinel Basin. Baraby and Sheeve had some score of Apache cattle bunched and were driving the stock away toward the west rim of the basin. This was just after sunup. Antone's voice grew sonorous, deep.

"My riders stopped this thing, this stealing. They did not fire the first shot. They were remembering my orders. Yet they could not stand aside and see our cattle stolen. These two at your feet began the shooting. The blood of my young men is hot. They have stood much—much. And so it was done. The fault is mine, not theirs. Somewhere, somehow, I have not been wise enough to have foreseen all that I should, and so, guarded against it. I will go with you. I have broken my word. I am ready to face the white man's law."

Reese Canby built a cigarette. The glow of the match cast a ruddy shine across the hard planes of his face. The match went out, and he was shadowy in front of Antone.

"All of the white man's law is not written, Antone," he said softly. "But it is there, just the same—the law that a man may shoot to protect his own life or his belongings. You have broken no law, nor your word, either. There is the earth. Put these two in it. They are not worth being remembered, so they will be forgotten by all men. Your young men did well. It is finished."

As he rode back to Cassadora, Canby figured out the picture. Sax Starke had sent Fox Baraby and Al Sheeve into Sentinel Basin on this small raid to draw the Apaches' attention to the lower end of the basin. This done, Harry Ide and his crowd were to strike higher up in a real raid. The furor over the big raid would cover up the significance of the little one, and thus two ends would be served. This little raid had taken place just after sunup, so Antone had said. Which meant that at that time, Sax Starke and Chelso De Lacca had no idea of what had taken place in the high piñon country. They did not know that he, Canby, had escaped, that Ide and his crowd had been cut to pieces and scattered.

The mills were grinding. The end of this thing was fast approaching. How would it be written? The answer to that was something no man could give. No man knew where his star hung, or when it would fall.

The lights of Cassadora lifted out of the night, and when Canby reached the edge of town, Sandy Foss's voice came out of the dark, "Reese?"

"Yeah, kid. What is it?"

"Starke and De Lacca are in town. Starke's over at Judge Marland's house, hollering his head off. He claims that Fox Baraby and Al Sheeve have disappeared, and he thinks the Apaches have done them in. He's demanding that Judge Marland send Mike Partman into Sentinel Basin to investigate."

"Then he still doesn't know what happened this morning up in the piñon country?"

"I guess not. He's acting righteous and injured as hell."

Canby slid out of the saddle. "Take care of my horse, kid. Starke's got a surprise coming."

"You can't handle everything alone," argued Sandy. "Some place your luck is bound to run out. I'm going along."

"Don't worry, kid. Starke won't start anything in front of Judge Marland."

Chapter XI
THE OPEN DOOR

There was a light going in Judge Marland's little study. His knuckles raised, ready to knock at the front door of the house, Reese Canby could hear voices, indistinct but angry. He had to knock three times before Judge Marland heard and answered.

Canby made a tall, dark shape in the outrush of light as the door swung back. Judge Marland, his eyes snapping with anger, exclaimed, "Canby! Glad to see you right now. Come on in."

Judge Marland's voice reached the study, and in there, at the sound of Canby's name, Sax Starke spun around, his face going white, looking trapped and desperate. Shadows of disbelief surged across his face. This couldn't be so. He had last left Reese Canby, tied hand and foot, in a renegade camp far up in the piñons, surrounded by wild, desperate men who would never have let the prisoner get away. To make sure of this fact, Sax Starke had put up a bargaining act, naming Canby as worth five thousand dollars to him. It was a bargain Starke never meant to keep. A bullet at the right time would be cheaper. But—Canby was here, in this house!

Sax Starke fought to get control of himself and

only partially succeeded, for as Reese Canby stepped into the study behind Judge Marland, his taunting, mirthless smile made a white line across his sun-blackened face.

"Don't tell me you're surprised, Starke," drawled Canby. "Things happen, you know. They did."

Judge Marland, not understanding this byplay, stared from one to the other. Starke licked his lips, his expression freezing. "What—what are you doing here?"

"Going to tell Judge Marland a long story. It's a crooked, contemptible story, but it's true. When I'm done, I'm quite sure the judge will agree with me that you and Chelso De Lacca have a big argument with the law coming up. It's an argument you're going to lose, Starke, because you've forfeited the regard and consideration of every decent man in this country. If you don't know the picture of bars in a prison window, you better start getting used to it. I think you'll be gazing at it for a long time—a very long time."

"That's—talk," said Starke jerkily. "The law—demands proof."

"Oh, I got plenty of that," said Canby coldly. "The evidence of dead men. Harry Ide's one of them. Newt Dyas is another. There's more. They're on your trail, Starke, those dead men are; you can't shake 'em. They'll stay with you until you're down in the shadows with them. And five thousand dollars, Starke! Is that all my hide was worth to you?"

A baffled, crimson light formed in Sax Starke's eyes. He was in the dark on so many things. Things he had carefully planned had fallen to pieces all around him. What was this Canby was saying about Newt Dyas and Harry Ide being dead—and more besides them? And Fox Baraby and Al Sheeve disappeared as though the earth had swallowed them? Yes, things had happened, for here was the proof of it. Right here in Reese Canby, standing before him, laughing at him in mockery.

By a tremendous effort, Starke pulled himself together. He moved toward the door, surprised that Canby made no move to stop him. "You're making the craziest talk I ever heard," said Starke. "Tell it to Marland if you want. You're making charges out of thin air. You can't back up a single one."

Starke was talking, just talking, trying to bluff this moment out. He wanted to get outside, find Chelso De Lacca, and plan something—anything!

He jerked the door open, plunged into the waiting dark. Reese Canby's mocking voice followed him.

"Won't do any good to run, Starke. You can't run far or fast enough to get away from this. There's dead men in the shadows. They're waiting for you."

The door slammed.

Judge Marland stared at Canby. "I'll be tee-totally crucified!" he exclaimed. "What's all this about, boy?"

"Sit down," said Canby. "It's a long story."

It was a full hour before Reese Canby left Judge Marland's cottage. When he did, he carried warrants with him calling for the arrest of Saxon Starke and Chelso De Lacca.

"Find Mike Partman and have him serve them," was the judge's instruction. "I'm glad we can end this thing by written laws, son. There's been violence enough."

Mike Partman wasn't at his office and, since Tippo Vance had refused to let Partman stay or drink in the Desert House, the best chance of finding him was in the Stag Head. As Canby started that way, Sandy Foss drifted up out of the shadows.

"Watch yourself, cowboy," he warned. "They're still in town."

"Good!" answered Canby. "Mike Partman won't have far to look."

Sandy drifted away again, down toward Bob Stent's store. Canby went into the Stag Head. Sure enough, Mike Partman was there. Canby drew him aside and handed him the warrants.

"Go get 'em, Mike. Your chore."

Partman gulped, then shrugged. "This'll blow the roof off. You should have showed up with these half an hour ago. They were both in here then. Now I suppose I'll have to ride clear out to Tepee after them."

"Don't think so, Mike. Sandy Foss said they're still in town somewhere."

Mike Partman went out. Canby looked around. Milt Parrall sat over at a poker table, head braced in his hands, staring at Canby. There was an empty glass at Milt's elbow. Milt looked very bad, haggard and unshaven, face bloated, eyes burning with a dull, sullen fire. Something seemed to be consuming the man from inside. Canby made as if to go over to him, but with Canby's first step, Parrall slid out of his chair, moved around the table, and headed for the door, lurching a little.

Canby shook his head in regret. Old friends were something a man liked to hang on to. Newt Dyas—dead. Milt Parrall was as good as dead, it seemed, as far as the old friendship was concerned. Well, he could thank Sax Starke and Chelso De Lacca for both these losses. Yes, and for the loss of Ponco and Dobe, the Apache boys he'd grown up with. But Starke and De Lacca were closer to the end of their trail than they figured. Mike Partman would go through with the chore of serving those warrants. Mike had bet on the wrong horse, and Starke had pushed him around, using him with contempt. Mike would be remembering that.

Canby went out into the night. He looked up at Billy Eustace's hotel, at the lights winnowing from window and open door. Bert Lanifee had said Chris was in town, would stay there until this range went quiet and settled again.

A swift yearning to see Chris, to hear her voice, swept over him. He headed for the hotel with eager steps. He nearly bumped into somebody who was out there in the dark, also staring at the hotel. It was Milt Parrall. A swift sympathy ran through Canby. Poor Milt. Breaking his whole world up, because he couldn't face the necessity of locking up his heart and saying goodbye to a dream. Refusing to steel himself to the understanding that this was a gamble a man had to take and to abide by the turn of the card, whether for or against him. A woman's heart was her own. It went here, or it went there. There was no alternative.

Milt seemed hardly to notice him. But abruptly, Milt's voice came, harsh yet sincere, "Don't step into that light, Reese!"

Canby stopped, spun around. Milt said, "Starke. Waiting for you. Over at the end of the hotel porch!"

Sax Starke's curse was like a raw whiplash across the dark.

"Parrall—you double-crossing—!"

The smash of Starke's gun drowned out the rest of his words.

The bullet told with a thud. Milt Parrall coughed and crumpled down.

Canby leaped past him, running straight at Starke, low and crouched. He picked up the shift of movement that was Starke, drove bullet after bullet. The round bloom of gun flame winked again and again. Canby kept driving in and shooting. Starke shot once more, wildly, then he went down in a slow, turning roll. Reese Canby stopped right over him, the hammer of his gun clicking on cylinders already fired.

The night, which had opened like a thunderclap, closed like another one. In the utter silence that fell, Canby could hear the blood pounding in his temples.

Then it was Chelso De Lacca's meaty, moist voice, incredibly malign, drifting in from the rear corner of the hotel.

"Too bad, Canby. You forgot there was two of us!"

"Count again, De Lacca," came Sandy Foss's hard cry. "Three of us!"

Sandy shot even as his yell rolled out.

Chelso De Lacca banged into the side of the hotel like a blind, mortally wounded buffalo. He bounced off, charged into it again. He fell over backward, boot heels drumming the ground. He died hard, did Chelso De Lacca—but he died!

Sandy came loping up through the night. He caught at Reese Canby's arm.

"Reese! You all right?"

"All right," answered Canby woodenly.

He turned, went back to Milt Parrall, gathered Milt up in his arms, and stumbled up onto the hotel porch with him.

They came running and crowding up from every side. People. They jostled and pushed, called questions back and forth. Canby paid them no attention, going on into the hotel, Milt Parrall in his arms.

Chris Lanifee was in there. So was Mary Stent. They'd been sitting in the parlor together, talking. Now Chris came toward Canby, white of face, eyes very big and dark with shock. She was looking at Milt Parrall hanging loose and still in Canby's arms.

"Reese!" she cried, her voice breaking slightly from the terror that shook her. "You didn't—not Milt! Oh, Reese—not you—!"

"Starke," answered Canby. "He was layin' for me. Milt warned me. Starke shot him. Get—Doc Snell—"

Chris turned away, pushing her hands against her face. Then she ran, calling for Doc Snell.

Mary Stent pulled at Canby's arm. "Over here, Reese—put him here."

Canby followed, put Milt Parrall down on the parlor sofa. Canby thought he was dead. All the front of Milt's shirt was soggy dark.

Doc Snell came running, his shirt half tucked

into his trousers. He'd been about to turn in for the night. Canby stepped back to give Doc room.

He swung his head, saw Billy Eustace and Sandy Foss holding the crowd outside the door. He turned back and said, "Well, Doc?"

"Still alive," said Doc tersely. "But—" Doc shook his head. He tipped a stimulant against Milt's lips. Most of it ran down Milt's jaw, then he coughed weakly and swallowed once.

His eyes opened, and he murmured—"Reese—?"

Canby dropped to a knee beside him. "Milt! Hang on, old settler. It's a tough ride—but hang on!"

Milt smiled faintly, shook his head weakly. "I'm tossed, cowboy." His eyes closed, but he went on speaking, substance fading slowly but definitely from his voice.

"That night—in front of the Stag Head, Reese? You said—you'd keep a door open. Is it—still open?"

"Still open, old partner. Always was open. Never could be any other way."

"That's good. Don't deserve it—but—it makes me—damn happy. Starke—how about—Starke?"

"Done for, Milt. I got him. De Lacca's done too. Sandy Foss got De Lacca."

Milt's smile deepened. He wagged his head slowly, as though enjoying a thought of his own.

"Joke's on them—two coyotes. Only two to

go now, Reese. Fox Baraby—Al Sheeve—only them two. Then you got—all five. The five who lynched—Ponco and Dobe. Couldn't get over—my part in that deal. It broke something in me. Yeah—the five of us. De Lacca—Al Sheeve—Fox Baraby—Jack Naile—me. Get Sheeve—Baraby—the slate's—clean—"

They didn't try to stop Milt from talking. This was something he had to say, to get rid of, a dark garment he had to shuck before he took the long ride.

Reese Canby thought he was gone, but Milt had a final word, a thinning whisper.

"Tell Chris—she picked—the right man. And keep the door open, boy—keep it open—"

That was all. Everything was gone now. Everything but memories.

Canby turned away blindly. Hands and voices tried to hold him back. He paid them no attention. He plunged through the door and out into the night. He grabbed the first horse he came to, swung astride, and rode—anywhere.

Dawn found him far out in the desert. Vague to the north, Pahvant Rim lifted, beginning to burn crimson across its long, running crest. The horse kept fighting the rein, wanting to turn north. Canby let it have its way. He recognized it as the one Sandy had been riding.

The desert was a blistering oven by the time

Canby saw the buildings of town lifting ahead. He swung east of it, keeping to the open range, driving for his own headquarters. He felt a million years old, all dry and wasted inside. His eyeballs seemed stiff in his head. He thought he would never have energy enough to give a damn about anything again.

No one was at headquarters. He stripped riding gear off the horse and turned it into the corral. He went into the bunkhouse, moving with a stiff, jarring step. He flattened out on the nearest bunk and told himself that sound sleep was something that would never come to him. He was wrong. It hit him like a club.

He awoke to the knowledge that people were around him. He pulled up on one elbow, blinked in surprise. They were all here. His crew, that he'd left with the herd up in the Chevrons. Somewhere outside a cow bawled. Men and cattle—they were home. Sandy Foss dropped down on the edge of the bunk.

"Scared hell out of us, wanderin' off the way you did," said Sandy gruffly. "I looked everywhere for you and finally decided to try the home ranch. Here you were. Right after that, the boys came in with the herd. I've told 'em everything, and they're all brokenhearted because they didn't arrive in time to get in on the fun."

"That's the wrong word, kid," said Canby.

"Sure," agreed Sandy quietly. "I know."

He talked with the men about the cattle, about the drive down from the Chevrons. Maybe it was the sleep, maybe it was the familiar faces about him, maybe the sight of his cattle, spreading across the flats along Telescope Creek, maybe it was something of all these. At any rate, he began to loosen up inside again, and the old swing came back to his shoulders.

He shaved and cleaned up. Evening was painting Pahvant Rim a luring powder-blue, quenching its slumberous fire. Canby took the trail to Trumpet headquarters. Just as he turned off into it, Sandy came cantering up behind. Canby reined in for a moment.

"Town, kid?"

"That's right." Sandy grinned. "I'll be usin' this trail considerable of evenings now."

The hard line of Canby's lips softened a trifle. "Give Mary my best."

Sandy said, "Sure," and rode on, whistling.

Well, thought Canby, that was the youth of it. Plenty of bounce. Things that were done were done. Nothing could change them. They were written in the book, and the page turned. The future beckoned, and youth rode, whistling.

Good Lord! He was thinking like an old man. Youth was his, too, and the future. That partnership proposition he'd thought of before—he'd have to talk that over with Sandy. The kid would need something bigger than just a puncher's job.

The lights of Trumpet reached out to him. A saddled horse shifted over as he swung his own mount up before the ranch house. Bert Lanifee's voice came down to him from the porch shadows, "Glad you rode in, Reese."

Mason Garr was with Bert. The crusty old cattleman stirred, puffed furiously on his stubby pipe.

"Want to say thanks, Reese—for myself and a lot of folks. You headed off something that could have been awful bad. Sorry I was so pigheaded for a time. No fool as blind as an old fool."

"It's a new day, Mason," said Canby. "We'll keep it so."

"About Fox Baraby and Al Sheeve. Any idea of what became of them?"

Canby did not answer for a moment. "They were dead the last time I saw them," he said finally. "Suppose we let it go at that."

"Sure," said Garr quickly, "sure. Somethin' else I wanted to talk to you about. That young cub puncher of yours, Sandy Foss. Strikes me him and Mary Stent got ideas."

"Mary," murmured Canby, "is one swell girl. And Sandy will do too."

"My own thought," agreed Mason Garr. "Me, I'm gettin' along. I ain't got kith or kin in the world. I got a pretty good ranch, but what good's it doin' me? Likewise, I'm gettin' tired. I need a foreman. I'd like to see my ranch house turned into a real home by somebody. I figger maybe Mary and Sandy could do that. Mary's always been my special favorite." He paused, cleared his throat. "I'd draw up a will. The ranch would go to them two kids. That way I'd figger I'd been some good in the world."

Canby dropped a hand on the old cattleman's shoulder. "The day Sandy and Mary make a match of it, I fire Sandy. And you can hire him. A go?"

"A go! Hah! Hum! You bet! If we was in town, I'd set up the drinks for everybody. A new day, you said, right?"

Canby looked around restlessly. Bert Lanifee smiled to himself in the dark.

"Try the corrals, Reese," he drawled. "Sometimes she goes out there to count the stars."

She was leaning against a corral fence, doing just that, when Canby found her. He hooked his elbows over the top rail and stood there beside her, saying nothing. Presently, she spoke.

"I've been wondering if we've a right to happiness, Reese, after all the sorrow left to others."

He stood so the starshine cast his lean, still face into a grave silhouette. She watched him closely.

"If everybody wondered that, Chris, then there'd be no happiness for anybody anywhere. I don't know why the totals cast up like they do. I don't know whether it's percentage, design, or what. All I know is that a man can't go back.

He's got to go ahead. And maybe he's the right to find happiness along the way. It's there for you and me if we want it, Chris."

He turned and looked down at her. Her fair hair was silver under the stars. All these years, from the days back on the old reservation. Kids then, skylarking with black-eyed Apache youngsters. All that the years had seen and made since, and now here they were, just the two of them. And the choice was theirs.

She reached out a hand and touched him. The contact seemed to draw her into his arms.

About the Author

L. (Llewellyn) P. Holmes (1895–1988) was born in a log cabin at Breckenridge, Colorado, atop the Rocky Mountains. After graduating high school, Holmes began to write for pulp magazines and was a major contributor to Leo Margulies's line of pulp publications. Beginning in the 1950s, he concentrated on writing western fiction and moved away from pulp writing. Holmes wrote westerns under his own name and the pseudonyms Matt Stuart, Dave Hardin, and Perry Westwood. He wrote more than fifty Western novels, including *Wild Summit* (as Matt Stuart) and *Delta Deputy*, and over six hundred magazine stories. He received the Spur Award from the Western Writers of America for his 1955 novel *Somewhere They Die*.

Center Point Large Print
600 Brooks Road / PO Box 1
Thorndike, ME 04986-0001 USA

(207) 568-3717

US & Canada:
1 800 929-9108
www.centerpointlargeprint.com